VAMPS

ELAINE LEE
Writer

WILLIAM SIMPSON
Artist

STUART CHAIFETZ
Colorist

CLEM ROBINS
Letterer

BRIAN BOLLAND
Cover Artist

VAMPS created by ELAINE LEE
and WILLIAM SIMPSON

ISBN 185286 627 6
FIRST EDITION: January 1996

Published by Titan Books Ltd, 42-44 Dolben Street, London SE1 OUP, under license from DC Comics.
Cover and compilation copyright ©1995 DC Comics. All Rights Reserved.

Originally published in single magazine form in VAMPS 1-6. Copyright © 1994-1995 DC Comics. All Rights Reserved. All characters, their distinctive likenesses
and related indicia featured in this publication are trademarks of DC Comics. The stories, characters, and incidents featured in this publication are entirely fictional.
Cover by Brian Bolland. Publication design by Eddie Ortiz.

Printed in Canada.
2 4 6 8 10 9 7 5 3 1

THERE WAS SOMETHIN' ABOUT IT FROM THE VERY FIRST RIDE.

MAYBE IT WAS THE BITE OF GREEN TOBACCO ON THAT WET CAROLINA WIND ...A WIND THAT KISSED ME COOL ON THE FACE AN' THRILLED OVER MY FLESH LIKE THE HANDS OF A HIGH SCHOOL LOVER.

MAYBE IT WAS THE FEEL OF FIFTY-SEVEN HORSEPOWER ROARIN' BETWEEN MY LEGS!

IT'S JUST UP AHEAD!

HEY, SKEETER! WHERE'S THE TURN-OFF?

...OR THE SMELL OF LEATHER AND WHISKEY...OF SUPER UNLEADED AND A HOT MALE PULSE ...

WE'D PICKED 'EM UP AT A ROAD HOUSE OUT ON 301.

SAID WE'D LEFT A PARTY ROLLIN' OUT AT SKEETER'S PLACE...

HANG A LEFT, BABY!

...A PARTY THAT NEEDED SOME MEN.

3

4

AS WITH LIONS, SO IT IS WITH US.

THE FEMALES HUNT...DRAGGING HOME THE WITLESS MEAT, SO THE PREENING MALE MAY FEAST.

HE WAS ON THE MEAT LIKE WHITE ON RICE. THE REST OF THE DINNER WAS BEATING A HASTY RETREAT. FAST FOOD...

...BUT, NOT FAST ENOUGH.

THE HOT BLOOD OF THE BIKER SHOT DOWN OUR MASTER'S THROAT, SENDING A BOLT OF CLEAR PAIN INTO MY GUT. FOR THE VAMPIRE, ABSTINENCE IS AGONY.

CARE TO JOIN ME?

AFTER YOU...

SO GREAT, IN FACT, THAT IT NEVER OCCURRED TO HIM THAT WE WOULD EVEN TRY IT.

AWWWWW... YOU'RE NOT LEAVIN' ME, SUGAR?

TO HOLD BACK...TO HUNGER WHILE ANOTHER FEEDS... IS AN ACHE BEYOND BEARING...

PLASMA, PLATELETS, AND LEUCOCYTES RUSHED DOWN HIS IDIOT GULLET...TRYING IN VAIN, TO FILL HIS BOTTOMLESS GREED...

...GLUTTING AND GORGING HIM...

: --urp!

...LEAVING HIM, FINALLY, BLOATED AND LOLLING ON THE GROUND, BLOOD DRUNK AND HELPLESS.

THAT WAS *DUMB*, DAVE, *REALLY DUMB!*

YEAH, DAVE ...IT'S SUPPOSED TO BE *LADIES* FIRST.

WE GOTTA TEACH YOU HOW TO BE A *MAN,* POPPI?

HUH?

TAKE HIM!

EVER SEE A MILK-DRUNK INFANT...JUST DONE NURSING...ITS MUSCLES USELESS, ITS EYES ROLLED BACK IN ITS HEAD? THAT'S THE LOOK OF A VAMPIRE AFTER A HEAVY FEED. HE'S WEAK THEN. VULNERABLE.

YOU CAN'T *DO* THIS! I *MADE* YOU! YOU'RE MY *BRIDES*!

IT'S BEEN A *LOUSY* MARRIAGE, DAVE...

...REALLY CO-DEPENDENT...

...YOU NEVER PICK UP YOUR SOCKS...

...WE GOT NOTHING IN COMMON, POPPI...

...SO, WE'RE DIVORCING YOU ...*NOW!*

EVEN AT HIS WORST, DAVE HAD THE STRENGTH OF TEN HUMAN MEN. WE, ON THE OTHER HAND, HAD TEAMWORK. AND, AS THE BRA-BURNERS USED TO SAY...

...SISTERHOOD IS POWERFUL!

THEY ALSO SAY, "YOU CAN'T KEEP A GOOD MAN DOWN"... AN' THAT WENT DOUBLE FOR A DIRTY PIECE LIKE DAVE.

HELL'S BELLS! EVEN A WARM-BLOODED, *LIVE* MAN'LL SUCK THE WIND OUT OF A GAL, IF SHE LETS HIM...

...BUT AT LEAST YOU GOT SOME *SEX* OUT OF IT. WITH DAVE, ALL WE EVER GOT WAS PROMISES AND SLEEPLESS NIGHTS AN' A WHOLE HELL-OF-A-LOT OF LIP!

I'LL MAKE YOU *PAY!* I'LL MAKE *YOU...*

UHH-HUHGN!

...ACK!

NOW SHUT UP AN' *DIE,* YOU SON OF A BITCH!

ICK!

WHADDA WE DO NOW?

SKEETER'S QUESTION WAS LIKE A HAMMER, WHACKING THE BACK OF MY BRAIN. I REALLY HADN'T *THOUGHT* PAST THE PART WHERE THE S.O.B. DIES.

WE HADN'T BEEN ALONE IN A MONTH OF BLUE MOONS... HAD ONLY *MADE* ONE DECISION SINCE *WE'D* BEEN MADE...AND THAT WAS DOIN' OLE DAVE IN.

GUESS WE BURY 'EM IN THE WOODS...SCATTER THE GRAVES... PUT A PIECE OF DAVE IN WITH EACH OF THE OTHERS...

...'CASE HE GETS ANY IDEAS ABOUT PULLIN' IT TOGETHER AN' WALKIN' OUT OF HERE.

TAKE THOSE BIKERS' LEATHERS FIRST. IF WE'RE GONNA RIDE THE SCOOTS, WE GOTTA LOOK LIKE WE NEED THE CLOTHING.

I FELT LIKE A MIDDLE-AGED DIVORCEE, OUT ON HER FIRST BLIND DATE. I KNEW I WAS SUPPOSED TO SAY SOMETHING, *BUT* I DIDN'T KNOW WHAT...

OKAY...   ...OKAY.

I'M *STARVING.*

...ahhhhhhh!

IT WAS REAL *SWEET* A' YOU TA LEND ME YOUR JACKET, BABY. COULDYA DO ME JUS' *ONE* MORE THING...?

NO... PLEASE...!

AWWWW, C'MON, HONEY...

...GIMME SOME *SUGAR!*

NO!

AIIIIEEEEEEEE!

WE BURNT ASPHALT, HEADIN' SOUTH AN' WEST, AWAY FROM DAVE AND OUR FORMER EXISTENCE. WE'D BURNT OUR BRIDGES, TOO, AND THERE'S NO GOIN' BACK NOW TA PICK UP THE PIECES...

...EVEN IF WE COULD *FIND* 'EM ALL.

DYSFUNCTIONAL AS IT IS, WE HAVE US A NEW FAMILY...

...AND ME.

SKEETER...

...SCREECH...

...MINK...

...WHIPSNAKE...

WHERE WE *HEADED,* HOWLER?

DON'T THINK IT MATTERS! WE JUST NEED TO PUT SOME *DISTANCE* BETWEEN US AN' HIM!

THAT'S THE TROUBLE WITH HAVIN' A VAMPIRE FOR AN ENEMY...EVEN A STONE-COLD *DEAD* ONE. YOU JUST NEVER CAN TELL WHEN HE MIGHT BE *POPPIN' UP.*

WHERE WE GON' SLEEP?

THERE'S FIVE OR SIX BONEYARDS IN EVERY BACKWATER TOWN IN AMERICA! WE'LL FIND US ONE!

IT'S A BIG COUNTRY -- AND ALL THE SOIL IS NATIVE.

HOT DAMN!

HEY, BLONDIE! WHYN'CHA PARK THAT MOTOR SCOOTER AN' TAKE A RIDE IN A REAL MACHINE?!

WHATCHA HAULING IN THAT RIG, HANDSOME?!

MEAT, BABY, AN' LOTS OF IT!

SOMETIMES THEY BEG FOR IT.

THE MAN SAYS HE'S HAULING MEAT!

SEEMS TO LIKE BLONDES. GO FOR IT!

"THE MEN WHO WOULD BE MEALS," WE CALL 'EM. AND WE'D JUST FOUND US ONE ON WHEELS. GOOD THING...

HE'S OUR TICKET TO DISTANCE AN' DOWN TIME. MINK'S THE MONEY. SHE'LL BOOK US A FIRST CLASS SLEEPER HEADED SOUTH...

GOT ROOM FOR A BIKE IN BACK?

SHIT, YEAH! GOT ROOM FOR EIGHT OR TEN!

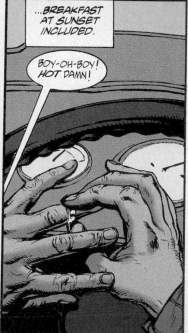

...BREAKFAST AT SUNSET INCLUDED.

BOY-OH-BOY! HOT DAMN!

SUNSET. THAT'S WHEN WE WAKE.

WE WAKE HUNGRY!

BUT IT'D BE DAMN FOOLISH FOR ALL OF US TO FEED AT ONCE. THAT LEAVES US SOFT ...VULNERABLE. ASK DAVE...

ONE OF US HAS TO GO WITHOUT...KEEP WATCH...PROTECT THE BLOOD-DRUNK PACK...

I'LL TAKE FIRST WATCH.

THE OTHERS HAVE TO *TRUST* HER.

THE TORMENT STARTS. I FEEL MY SISTERS FEEDING, SUCKING THE FIRE OUT OF THE MAN...FEEL LIKE A GREAT HAND PUSHING AND RIPPING INTO MY BURNING GUT...

...TEARING THE VERY ENTRAILS OUTTA ME, INCH BY BLOODY INCH. FIRE! COLD FIRE!

PAINFUL AS IT IS...A VAMP IS NEVER STRONGER THAN WHEN SHE'S GOT THE HUNGER ON.

CAN'T LAST LONG, THOUGH.

BEFORE THE NIGHT IS OVER, I'LL HAVE TO FEED.

BEFORE THE NIGHT IS OVER...

HOOOOOOOO!

YOU READY, GORGEOUS?

HIT ME, BABY!

GO SKEETER!

BUD

"LADIES NITE" IS WHAT THE SIGN SAYS, AND "LADIES DRINK FREE."

GOOD THING.

ONE UPSIDE-DOWN MARGARITA, GOIN' DOWN!

SKEETER'S PUTTING ON QUITE A SHOW. THAT'S GOOD, TOO.

THEY WON'T REMEMBER WHO DANCED WITH THE RED-HEADED COWBOY...HAD THE HALF-MOON SCAR NEAR HIS LEFT EYE.

CAN YOU STILL STAND UP?

...JUST PASSIN' THROUGH.

I WAS WEANED ON JACK'N'GINGER, SUGAR. AIN'T NOTHIN' HERE CAN MAKE ME DRUNK BUT YOU!

18

WHYN'CHA HANG AROUND? WE COULD HAVE US SOME RED-HEADED BABIES!

...SOMETIME TOMORROW...WHEN THE SUN COMES UP, BUT HE DON'T COME DOWN FOR COFFEE AND EGGS.

THAT'S NOT IN THE CARDS FOR ME, RED, BUT...I TELL YA...

THEY'LL TRY TO REMEMBER... "WHO'D HE LEAVE WITH LAST NIGHT?" THAT'S WHAT THEY'LL SAY WHEN THEY FIND HIM...

...I'M REALLY RUNNIN' ON EMPTY. WHADAYA SAY WE GO OUT FOR A BITE?

OKAY...BUT ONLY IF IT'S ON ME!

I WOULDN'T HAVE IT ANY OTHER WAY.

THEY'LL LOOK AND THEY'LL FIND HIM AND THEY'LL TRY...

...BUT THEY'LL ONLY REMEMBER THE GAL ON THE BAR WITH HER SKIRT HITCHED UP TO HEAVEN.

HEY, LUCKY! GOIN' OUT FOR SOME CHOW, Y'ALL WANNA COME ALONG?

THAT'S OKAY. I'LL REMEMBER YOU, RED.

THAT YOUR NAME? LUCKY?

THAT'S RIGHT! AN' TONIGHT, FOR ONCE, I'M FEELIN' THAT WAY! YOU HUNGRY?

NO THANKS, HONEY, I ALREADY ATE. AND, YOU KNOW...

...I THINK YOU ARE LUCKY!

COLD BEER

WET T-SHIRT

YEEEE-HAH!

HOO! FRESH AIR!

BEAUTIFUL NIGHT!

I REMEMBER THEM ALL.

TUESDAY is LADIES NITE! Ladies drink FREE!

I JUST LOVE ME A BIG, STRONG MAN. I COULD JUST LOVE YOU T'DEATH, DARLIN'!

ESDAY LADIES NITE

JESUS! YOU'RE STRONG FOR BEIN' SUCH A TINY LITTLE THING.

MMMMMMM...NOW *LOOK* AT ME, BABY... I NEED TO SEE MYSELF IN YOUR EYES...

I ONLY HAVE EYES FOR YOU, DARLIN'!

I CAN *SEE* THAT, LUCKY. NOW COME 'ERE AN' GIMME SOME SUGAR!

OUCH!

C'MON!

LEAVE THE MAN ALONE, SKEETER!

WE GOTTA GO ...*NOW!*

YOU'RE SWEET AS CANDY, BABY. I'LL LOOK YOU UP, IF I'M EVER BACK THIS WAY.

uh...OKAY? I THINK...

YOU TAKE TOO MANY CHANCES, MOMMI. WHY YOU SIP THIS GUY RIGHT OUT IN PUBLIC AN' YOU'RE NOT EVEN HUNGRY?

SHE JUST HAS TO TAKE A PINCH OF EVERY CHOCOLATE IN THE BOX.

I CAN'T HELP IT-- I'M SOUTHERN! IT'S FUN T'TEASE 'EM...THE CUTE ONES ANYWAY.

AN' THEY TASTE SO-O-O-O GOOD, WHEN THEIR BLOOD'S IN AN UPROAR.

YOU TELL 'EM, SWEETIE!

SCREECH IS SUCH A SMART-ASS. I DON'T KNOW WHY DAVE DECIDED TO TURN HER.

WHIPSNAKE THINKS SHE'S QUEEN A' TH' DAMNED!

WHICH WAY DID HOWLER GO?

LOOK! WAY OUT OVER THERE!

THE NIGHT SIGHS AND MOANS...THE EARTH, SHE ROLLS UNDER IT. ALL HIS STROKIN', SEE...IT MOVES HER...AN' SHE PITCHES AN' STRAINS, HEAVIN' HER GREAT HIPS TOWARD THE ROCKING SKY. I CAN HEAR THE WORLD BREATHE...BREATHIN' HEAVY.

I THOUGHT YOU WERE HUNGRY?

I AM, BABY...FOR YOU.

THE BOY-MAN BREATHES, TOO...BREATHES AN' POUNDS AN' SWELLS... AN I'M CAUGHT BY HIS CURRENT, CARRIED UNDER ON WAVES OF SCENT AN' HEAT...

...HIS LIVE HEART DRUMMIN' IN MY COLD, DEAD CHEST.

I'LL TAKE YOU, NOW...

SO...HUNGRY...

LIFE AN' DEATH...DEATH AN' LIFE...GRINDIN' GROINS TOGETHER LIKE TWO GREEN KIDS IN A SLOW DANCE GROPE. DANCE TO THE BEAT AN' THE HEAT AN' THE BEAT. HIS HEART... STRONG HEART!

THE GREAT YOUNG HEART THUNDERS ITS FINAL SONG... PUMPING THE HOT RED LIFE INTO MY THROAT... FIRING AND FILLING ME... WILD, BABY... NEED YOU WILD!

NEED IT... NEED I GIVE IT TO ME, BABY! DON'T STOP NOW! DON'T STOP! DON'T...

AHHOOOOOOOOO

PULLED UP BY THE SHORT HAIRS AN' HANGIN' THE KNIFE-SHARP EDGE OF A FEED! DAMN THEM! DAMN!

LEFT ME ALL PUMPED UP AN' NOWHERE T'GO AND DAMNING THEIR UNDEAD FEMALE SOULS.

RRRRRHHH!

LET'S SPLIT, SWEETIE! CAN'T MISS OUR BEAUTY SLEEP!

KNEES DON'T WORK...

CAN YOU RIDE?

YEAH...

SO LONG, BUCKEROO. NO RED-HEADED BABIES FOR YOU.

STAY BETWEEN ME AND SCREECH...

...JUST 'TIL THE ROAD STOPS WOBBLING!

♪ AS I-EE WALKED DO-OWN THE STREETS OF LA-RE-DO! AS I WALKED OUT IN LA-RE-DO ONE DAY...

...NO BABIES AT ALL- FOR RED-HEADED COWBOYS...

...AN' NONE FOR WHORES AND MONSTERS, THE LADIES OF THE NIGHT!

I SPIED A YOUNG COWBOY ALL WRAPPED IN WHITE LINEN... ♪

SHUT UP, SKEETER! YOU DON'T SING FOR SHIT!

WHORES FEED ON LOVE, AND MONSTERS ON LIFE, AND MAMAS... FOR LOVE... LET LIFE FEED ON THEM!

...ALL WRAPPED IN WHITE LINEN AN' COLD AS THE CLAY! ♪♪

YOU STEADY NOW, SWEETIE?

YEAH, I'M GREAT!

I GOT NO LIFE TO GIVE... NO LOVE, NEITHER.

...JUST GREAT.

THEY TOOK THE LOVE FROM ME NEARLY FOUR YEARS AGO.

YOU CAN'T DO THIS! YOU HAVE NO RIGHT!

THAT'LL BE DECIDED IN COURT, MISS.

DO YOU HAVE ANYTHING TO SAY FOR YOURSELF?

THERE WAS NO WORK, YOUR HONOR. I HAD TO TAKE CARE OF HIM AND IT'S LEGAL IN NEVADA. I NEEDED MONEY TO TAKE CARE OF HIM. DO YOU THINK ANYONE WOULD CHOOSE THAT KIND OF WORK?

THEY DID IT NICE AND LEGAL...

SO NICE AND LEGAL, THERE WAS NO UNDOIN' IT. THEY TOOK HIM...

...JUST BEFORE THAT BASTARD, DAVE...HE TOOK MY LIFE...WHAT WAS *LEFT* OF IT.

LET ME DIE...
LET ME DIE...
LET ME DIE...

YOU DON'T WANNA DIE, BABE.

WHAT?!

YOU JUST WANNA *HURT* 'EM, DON'T YOU? I CAN HELP YOU WITH THAT, BABE. I CAN MAKE IT BETTER.

THEY ALWAYS SAY THAT, DON'T THEY? *MEN*...THE LIVING AND THE DEAD ONES, TOO.

LET DAVE MAKE IT BETTER...

BELIEVE AT YOUR OWN RISK.

WELL, DAVE'S DEAD AND THERE ARE OTHER MONSTERS TO BE SLAIN...

SKREEECH

25

THE HUMAN KIND...THE JUDGES... THE LOVE KILLERS! BUT THE MONSTERS'LL HAVE TO WAIT.

FIRST COMES SLEEP. THE SUN'S A HARD BITCH AN' I'M GOIN' *DOWN* IN THE WORLD...DOWN SIX FEET.

DO A ONE-NIGHT STAND WITH ANY JOE STIFF HAS ROOM IN HIS BOX!

BUT, COME NEXT SUNSET...

MOVE OVER, WILLYA, SUGAR?

HE DON'T HEAR YOU, SKEETER, AN' I DON'T WANNA HEAR YOU!

EPILOGUE...

THANKS FER CALLIN', ED.

NO PROBLEM, AMIGO...

TELL YA TH' GOSPEL, HANK... I'M HAPPY T'HAVE TH'COMPANY ON THIS ONE. HOPE YA AIN'T JUST HAD LUNCH.

ED, WHAT YOU GON' SHOW ME THAT I AIN'T ALREADY...?

GEEZE-AWMIGHTY-CHRISTOPHER!

Next: WIND RIDERS

WE'D HAD A HELL OF A RIDE SINCE WE DONE IN DAVE, AN' LEFT HIS BUTT-UGLY UNDEAD FLESH UNDERNEATH THE CAROLINA SOIL...

...IN FIVE DIFFERENT UNMARKED GRAVES.

I'M A OLE COW HAND! FRUM TH' RIO GRAND! ♪

HEY, HOWLER! WHAT'S THE PLAN?

NGL PIG 3

NOW WE WERE MASTERLESS AN' BURNIN' RUBBER DOWN THE ROAD TO HELL.

WE NEED NEW PLATES! THE COPS'LL BE LOOKIN' FOR THESE BIKES!

BUT MY LEGS AIN'T BOWED! ♪ AN' MY BOD AIN'T TANNED!

I REALLY HATE THAT I'VE LOST MY TAN!

CAIN'T SIT A HORSE, CAIN'T ROPE OR SHOOT! ♪ BUT, I RIDE TH' RANGE ON' M' HARLEY SCOOT! DRINKIN' HUMAN BLOOD FROM A COWBOY BOOT!

...WHO'D DRINK ANYTHING FROM A BOOT?

GROSS ME OUT, SKEETER...

YIPPE-YI-YO-KI-YAY-AAY! ♪

THAT'S THE WAY I'VE ALWAYS RUN. EVEN BEFORE! I WAS HOWLER... BEFORE I WAS VAMP.

WEST... MAYBE DOWN TO VEGAS. I'LL KNOW WHEN I GET THERE.

WHICH WAY ARE WE HEADING?!

WEST!

HOW CAN YOU DO THIS? HOW CAN YOU JUST RUN AWAY?

NOW, I'M SURE OF ONLY TWO THINGS...ONE IS THAT I'VE DIED *TWICE* ALREADY...

HOLD YA HORSES, LI'L LADY, I'M COMIN'!

BAM BAM BAM

MOTORCYCLE...BROKE DOWN...HAD TO PUSH IT...NEED TO CALL FOR HELP...

AWRIGHT...AWRIGHT...JUSSA MINUTE NOW, HONEY!

...THE OTHER IS THAT, *BECAUSE* I'VE DIED TWICE, A WHOLE LOTTA *OTHER* FOLKS'LL DIE.

OTHER FOLKS...LIKE A NIGHT WATCHMAN FOR THE TEXAS DMV. I SMELL THE MAN'S FEAR...

AIIIEEEE!

TAKE THE WATCH, SCREECH. YOU CAN'T WORK THAT *COMPUTER* IF YOU'RE BLOOD-DRUNK.

...FEEL HIS PANICKED, PUMPIN' HEART...HAMMERING...POUNDING! NOT LIKE THE *YOUNG* HEARTS...NOT LIKE THE COWBOY'S...

...JUST A WEARY LITTLE CHOO-CHOO T'HAUL MY FREIGHT ...PUSH ME UP 'N' OVER THAT HILL... CHUG...CHUG...CHUG...

x

32

GALLAGHER! GALLAGHER, WHERE *ARE* YA, SON? SOUNDS LIKE YOU'RE IN A *CAVE* OR SUMP'M!

WE'RE TALKIN' ON A SPEAKER PHONE, SIR, AN' WE'RE IN TH' MORGUE, SO IT KINDA HAS THAT ECHO. THERE'S SOMEBODY HERE WANTS T'TALK TO YA.

THE CHIEF'S GOT A FEW QUESTIONS FOR YA, MR. BEDGOOD. BUT FIRST OFF, I'D LIKE T'SAY I'M REAL SORRY 'BOUT YOUR BROTHER-IN-LAW.

YEAH... EVEN *THAT* SUMBITCH DIDN' DESERVE T'DIE LIKE *THAT!* JEEZUS! THEY SAID ALL THE DUMB SUMBITCH'S *BLOOD'D* BEEN *DRAINED* OUT!

MR. BEDGOOD...? THIS IS CHIEF DWAYNE BRADSHAW OF THE AUSTIN POLICE. I'M DOWN HERE AT THE MORGUE WITH YER P.I. FRIEND.

YES, SIR... HE WAS HANGIN' FROM A *MEAT HOOK* IN 'IS *FRIGERATOR TRUCK,* AN' THA'S WHAT WE WANNA AST YOU ABOUT, MR. BEDGOOD. WE NEED T'KNOW HAS YOUR COMPANY EVER GOT ANY CRANK CALLS FROM ANY A' THOSE *VEGETARIANS...* OR *ANIMAL* RIGHTS WACKOS?

YOU TRYIN' T'TELL ME SOME *CARROT EATER* CUT 'IS THROAT?

ALL I'M SAYIN' IS IT'S POSSIBLE. I'M SURE YOU KNOW HOW *CRAZY* THEM TYPES CAN GET.

I SURE AS HECK DO! THEM PAIN-IN-THE-TAIL "BAMBI SAVERS" GIMME PLENTY A' GRIEF, BUT... *HELL'S BELLS!* MOST OF 'EM SOONER *SHOOT* THEIRSELVES THAN SWAT A GNAT! YOU BUYIN' THIS, GALLAGHER?

NO, SIR. I'M NOT. AN' I GOT SOME INFORMATION I'D LIKE T'RUN BY YA. THEY FOUND SOME MOTOR OIL IN THE BACK OF THE TRUCK... AND TIRE MARKS ON THE HIGHWAY... LIKE SOMEBODY'D PEELED RUBBER AWAY FROM THE TRUCK... MORE THAN *ONE* SOMEBODY.

WHAT'RE YOU SAYIN', MR. GALLAGHER?

DID YOUR BROTHER-IN-LAW HAVE A MOTORCYCLE, MR. BEDGOOD?

A MOTOR-CYCLE?!

...OR DID HE EVER PICK UP HITCHHIKERS?

HITCHHIKERS! OF ALL TH' GOLDERN STUPID GODDAM STUPID SUMBITCHIN' DUMB THINGS T'DO, GODDAM!? STUPID HIDE!

FOUND ON BODY--
CONDOMS
PLASTIC COMB
KEYS
5 DOLLARS + 75 CENTS
ONE GOLD WEDDING BAND found in right front jeans pocket
INDIANS CAP
PACK CAMEL CIGS

HOLD ON A MINUTE, MR. BEDGOOD...

MAKE MY SISTER A GODDAM WIDOW GODDAM IT!

HEY, CHIEF...THAT SKIN THEY FOUND UNDER THE DEAD TRUCKER'S FINGERNAILS? IT'S FROM A DEAD PERSON ...LONG TIME DEAD! I MEAN, LIKE A CORPSE! WEIRD AS BAT SHIT, AIN'T IT?

HELLO? HELLO? GOLDERN IT! WHAT'S THE HELL'S GOIN' ON!

BESIDES THAT, THERE WAS SOME KINDA COSMETIC STUFF... SKIN CREAM OR SOME-THIN'...THEY DON'T KNOW EXACTLY, YET, BUT THEY'RE WORKIN' ON IT.

DO ME A FAVOR, ED, AN' TELL 'EM T' FIND OUT IF IT CAME FROM ONE A THEM HEALTH FOOD COMPANIES THAT DON'T TEST THE SHIT ON BUNNIES...WHATTA THEY CALL IT?

YOU KNOW, GALLAGHER...

...GALLAGHER?

GALLAGHER? GALLAGHER!

HANK? HEY, OLE BUDDY!

GODDANG IT! WHERE'D HE GO?!

RING! RING!

C'MON, JUDY...ANSWER TH' PHONE, DARLIN'...

CONDOMS--
RING IN POCKET--
HITCHHIKERS?

HEY, JUDY, YOU BURNIN' HUNK A' FEMALE LOVE! NEED YA T'CHECK SOME-THIN' FOR ME...LOOK FOR CRIMES HAVIN' TO DO WITH MOTOR-CYCLES. LOOK EVERY-WHERE, BUT START WITH NORTH CAROLINA ...ANYTHING BETWEEN THERE AN' TEXAS.

NAWWW-- COPS HADN'T GOT A CLUE.

WE'RE ON OUR OWN WITH THIS ONE, HONEY.

34

LONE STAR HOG

SWEET HONEY LUCK RIDES WITH US TONIGHT. SPOTTED A HARLEY DEALER OUT ON 409, WEST OF AUSTIN. SCREECH TOOK OUT THE SECURITY SYSTEM. WHIPSNAKE'S HAVIN' A TALK WITH THE LOCKS.

MY COUSIN, LITTLE EDDIE, TAUGHT ME HOW TO DO THIS...

...HE'S SERVING EIGHT-TO-TEN UPSTATE.

WHIPSNAKE'S THE MECHANIC OF THE PACK. HER DADDY RAN A GARAGE CALLED SEVEN DAUGHTERS BACK IN NYC. WHIPSNAKE'S THE SEVENTH.

THERE!

KLICK

SHE'S GOOD WITH HER HANDS.

TIME TO REPLACE THOSE DEAD BIKERS' RIDES WITH SCOOTS A TOUCH HARDER TO TRACE.

GEEZE, LOUISE! LOOKIT ALL THESE BEAUTIFUL BIKES!

THIS ONE WILL DO FOR ME.

PURPLE, MINK? AND CUSTOM? BETTER MATCH THE MAKE AND COLOR TO THE REGISTRATION, DON'TCHA THINK?

HEY! WHAT'RE YOU BITCHES DOIN' IN HERE?

THERE'S THAT WORD AGAIN!

JEEZUS!

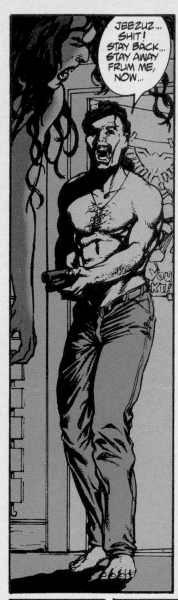

JEEZUZ... SHIT! STAY BACK... STAY AWAY FRUM ME, NOW...

KA BLAM

KA BLAM KA BLAM

KA BLAM

AGHHH!

WE LIVE IN TIMES OF LITTLE FAITH. MOSTLY, WE LIKE IT THAT WAY.

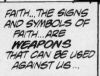

FAITH...THE SIGNS AND SYMBOLS OF FAITH...ARE **WEAPONS** THAT CAN BE USED AGAINST US...

UGHN!

...BUT ONLY IF A PERSON **BELIEVES.**

THIS ONE DOESN'T.

FUH-BUM -PUH BUM-PUH BUM -PUH BUM -UH-BUH

BLOOD HEALS.

WE LET WHIPSNAKE DRINK.

SHE NEEDS IT.

MORE THAN WE DO.

LOOK WHAT THAT SONOFABITCH DID TO MY LEATHER!

I THINK IT'S ONLY FAIR THAT HE BUYS US ALL *NEW* OUTFITS.

IT'S THE LEAST HE COULD DO!

WE NEED TO HURRY. I HAVE TO FEED SOON.

SOMEBODY HELP WHIPSNAKE! THE REST OF YOU... HELP ME TEAR UP SOME T-SHIRTS... MAKE SOME FUSES. WE CAN'T LET ANYBODY FIND *ANYTHING* HERE.

THE HARLEYS BELONGIN' TO THE FIVE DEAD BIKERS WOULD HAVE TO BE DESTROYED...ALONG WITH THE REST OF THE SHOP. WE WOULDN'T WANT ANYONE KNOWIN' THAT FIVE BRAND-*NEW* BIKES WERE MISSIN' AN PROBABLY OUT ON THE ROAD.

THE SUN CAME OUT THAT NIGHT, AN' WE SAT WATCHIN' IT...

...FROM A SAFE DISTANCE...

GUESS WE SHOULD GO, HUH?

YEAH...IN A MINUTE.

ALL THOSE LOVELY MACHINES! IT'S KINDA SAD...

BEEN A LONG TIME SINCE I'VE SEEN ANYTHING SO PRETTY AN' WARM.

AIIIE! SKEETER, ARE YOU CRYING AGAIN?

I CAN'T HELP IT!

YOU GOTTA HELP IT, MOMMI! IT GIVES US AWAY!

VAMPS AREN'T USUALLY MUCH ON CRYIN'. ONCE YOU GET USED TO KILLIN' ON A NIGHTLY BASIS, THERE AIN'T A WHOLE LOT LEFT FOR YOU TO CRY ABOUT...

...AND THE TEARS, WHEN THEY COME, ARE THE COLOR OF BLOOD. SKEETER'S A SOFT TOUCH.

UP YOURS!

I CAN UNDERSTAND HER FEELINGS, THOUGH. SOME WICKED TRANSPORT WENT UP IN THAT FIRE!

WHO THE HELL IS *THIS*, AT THREE IN THE DAMN MORNIN'?!

I DON'T THINK YOU *MISS* ME, JUDY! ARE YOU IN BED WITH THAT NO-GOOD SALOON-KEEPER? I'LL HAVE T'KILL 'IM...

...THE *WIVES* A' THOSE FIVE GUYS I TOLD YA ABOUT? THEY TOLD THE COPS THEIR MEN WENT OUT FOR A BEER AN' *NEVER CAME BACK!*

HANK GALLAGHER, YOU QUIT SWEET-TALKIN' ME AN' LISTEN...

WOULDN'T BE THE FIRST TIME A MAN DONE THAT.

ALL FIVE OF 'EM?

HEY, HANK! GOTTA GO!

JUST A MINUTE, ED...

IF YOU WANNA SEE THAT *BODY*, WE GOTTA GO *NOW!*

CALL YOU BACK LATER, SWEETHEART.

NOT TONIGHT, YOU DON'T!

GOT SOME-THIN' FOR YOU TOO, ED.

WE MAY BE LOOKIN' FOR FIVE BIKERS...

...DISAPPEARED IN NORTH CAROLINA AT JUST THE RIGHT TIME...ON THEIR HARLEYS. A COUPLE OF THE WIVES REPORTED 'EM MISSIN'.

BIKERS? AN' THEY'RE DRAININ' THE BLOOD OUTTA FOLKS?

SURE YOU *WANNA* FIND 'EM, HANK?

LORD, I *HOPE* NOT! MOSTA THOSE GUYS'RE *BIG!* BIG LIKE YOU *DON'T* GET EATIN' CELERY JUICE AND TOFU!

A BAR'S A GOOD PLACE FOR A GAL TO FIND A DRINK...'SPECIALLY OUR PARTICULAR KIND OF POISON.

GO, WHIPSNAKE! SHOW 'EM WHO'S BOSS!

THAT LI'L GAL'S GIVIN' MULE A RUN FER 'IZ MONEY!

DON'T LET US DOWN NOW, MULE!

DRUNKS GOT NO MEMORY, BUT JUST TO MAKE SURE, WHIPSNAKE'S PROVIDING THE SHOW TONIGHT...

...WHILE SCREECH SCARES UP HER DINNER DATE.

GO SLOW, GIRL...DON'T SHOW 'EM TOO MUCH... DON'T LET THE BEAST OUT.

HOW LONG YOU BEEN RIDIN'?

RIDING WHAT, HANDSOME?

YOU GOT LESS CONTROL THAN THE REST OF US, MOMMI. PLEASE...

GO! GO! GO! GO!

EVENIN', GENTLEMEN...

...PLAY IT SMART.

...AND LADIES.

SLAM

40

SCREECH'S DATE PLAYS IT SAFE--MUST HAVE SOME PROBLEM WITH THE LAW.

HAW HA HA

WE'RE LOOKIN' FOR SOME BIKERS.

WELL, YER SHIT OUTTA LUCK, OFFICER. NO BIKERS AROUND HERE!

VERY FUNNY...

WHUSSA MATTER? SOME BRO RIDE PAST YA WITHOUT A HELMET?

WE'RE LOOKIN' FOR FIVE BIKERS...PROB'LY RIDIN' HARLEYS WITH CAROLINA PLATES...WANTED IN CONNECTION WITH A COUPLA MURDERS. SEEN ANYBODY LIKE THAT?

IF WE HAD, WE'D CERTAINLY TELL YOU ABOUT IT, OFFICER.

THINK WE CAN TAKE ALL OF 'EM?

SHHHH!

DON'T THINK I'VE SEEN YOU GALS AROUND THESE PARTS. WHERE'D YOU RIDE IN FROM?

THIS HERE'S MY OLE LADY, SO YOU CAN JUST START EATIN' YER HEART OUT! THESE GALS BEEN RIDIN' WITH US FOR WEEKS... MET 'EM AT THAT RALLY IN SAN DIEGO.

YOU SURE ABOUT THAT?

TELL THE MAN 'BOUT MY TATTOO, BABY.

HE'S GOT A GREAT BIG BUMBLEBEE TATTOOED RIGHT ON THE END OF HIS

SHE'S TELLIN' IT TRUE, OFFICER! LADY ARTIST IN L.A. DONE IT FOR ME, HERE...

...I'LL SHOW YOU!

FORGET IT, BUDDY. I BELIEVE YA.

IF YOU SEE ANY-BODY COME THROUGH WITH NORTH CAROLINA PLATES...

...WE'D LIKE IT IF YOU'D GIVE US A CALL.

EVENIN'.

SLAM

YOU GIRLS AVOIDIN' THE LAW?

WHY? YOU FIGURE ON TURNIN' US IN?

HOW TO DISAPPEAR
A MANUAL FOR GOING UNDERGROUND

NAWWW, NOT A BIT. HERE, TAKE THIS...

...IT'LL TELL YOU HOW TO GET ID... SOCIAL SECURITY CARDS... HOW TO BE WHO YOU NEED TO BE.

MUCH OBLIGED, FRIEND.

WE GOTTA STICK TOGETHER, DON'T WE?

YOU'RE RIGHT.

WHERE YOU GOIN' SCREECH?

SEE IF MY MAN'S OUTSIDE...

SEE YA 'ROUND, BOYS!

YOU CAN RIDE BEHIND ME ANY DAY OF THE WEEK, SWEETHEART!

WE DON'T RIDE BEHIND, BABY!

THAT LI'L GAL'S GOT BALLS!

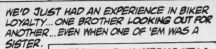

WE'D JUST HAD AN EXPERIENCE IN BIKER LOYALTY... ONE BROTHER LOOKING OUT FOR ANOTHER... EVEN WHEN ONE OF 'EM WAS A SISTER.

THERE'S NOTHIN' *WRONG* WITH A LITTLE MALE PROTECTION, WHEN YOU CAN *GET* IT

THEN WHYN'T CHOO GO BACK AN' KNIT DAVE TOGETHER, MOMMI?

WHYN'T *CHOO* SLITHER BACK UNDER YOUR ROCK?

SHE'S RIGHT, SKEETER. YOU THINK HE'D HAVE COME TO THE RESCUE IF WHIPSNAKE HADN'T LET HIM *WIN*?

THOSE GUYS ARE ONLY GOOD FOR ONE THING.

SO, ARE WE JUST GONNA LEAVE, OR DO WE ORDER TAKE-OUT?

I BEEN THINKIN' ABOUT THAT.

IN A WAY, WE HAD A LOT IN COMMON WITH THESE GUYS. WE WERE MISFITS AN' OUTLAWS, IN LOVE WITH FREEDOM AND THE OPEN ROAD. OF COURSE, THE SIMILARITIES ENDED THERE...

...MOST BIKERS PREFERRIN' A COLD BREW TO BLOOD SERVED AT BODY TEMP.

I SAY WE LEAVE THIS PLACE AS WE FOUND IT AND WE MAKE A PACT. NO MORE BIKERS, NO BIKE DEALERS, NO MECHANICS...

VERY *EASY* FOR YOU TO SAY. YOU'VE EATEN.

I COULD SEE I HAD MY WORK CUT OUT FOR ME, CONVINCIN' FOUR FEMALE VAMPS THAT *ANY* HUMAN MALE WAS SOMETHING MORE'N MEAT.

LISTEN... WHEREVER WE GO, WE GOTTA ALWAYS BE LOOKIN' OVER OUR SHOULDER LOOKIN' FOR THAT BASTARD DAVE AN' FOR *ANYTHING* ELSE THAT KNOWS WHAT WE ARE.

IF WE KEEP FAITH WITH THE BIKERS... BECOME PART OF THE BROTHERHOOD. WE SUDDENLY GOT TEN THOUSAND EXTRA EYES. WE'LL BE SAFER FOR IT. IF, ON THE OTHER HAND, WE KEEP *DRINKIN'* BIKERS... WORD WILL GET AROUND. THOSE EYES WILL TURN ON *US*! TRUST ME!

YOU ALL AGREE?

SURE.

LET'S DO IT.

GEE... I DON'T *KNOW*. WHADDA YOU THINK...

...SCREECH? WHERE'S SCREECH?

44

EVEN IN TIMES OF LITTLE FAITH, THERE ARE THOSE WHO BELIEVE.

I'M STANDING HERE. I'M PRAYING. I'M STANDING IN THE EAST. I'M STANDING IN THE SOUTH. I'M STANDING IN THE WEST. I'M STANDING IN THE NORTH. I'M THANKING THE CREATOR, FOR THIS MY LIFE...

...GRANDFATHER, I'M STANDING HERE. I'M ASKING SPIRIT FOR GUIDANCE...

THE SYMBOLS OF FAITH ARE WEAPONS THAT CAN BE USED AGAINST US.

A CROSS IS JUST ONE. THERE ARE OTHERS.

OF COURSE, THERE ARE WAYS OF DISARMING YOUR VICTIM.

AHHH?!

I AM YOUR VISION!

I'M CRYING FOR A VISION...

SKREEEE

45

I WOULD TELL YOU OF YOUR FUTURE...COME... COME CLOSER...

IF YOU ARE FROM *SPIRIT* THEN YOU KNOW THAT I CAN'T...

...I CAN'T CROSS MY PRAYER TIES.

IT'S... FORBIDDEN...

PERHAPS *SPIRIT* IS TESTING YOUR COURAGE...YOUR WILLINGNESS TO STEP INTO THE UNKNOWN?

PERHAPS THE REWARD WOULD BE GREAT? AS GREAT AS YOUR LEAP OF FAITH?

THE THING ABOUT *FAITH* IS...

...YOU HAVE TO KEEP IT.

EAT AN' RUN. THAT'S THE ROAD WE'VE CHOSEN.

THAT BOY HAD PROTECTION! THEY'LL FIND HIM AND THERE WILL BE A STINK!

WE GOTTA LAY LOW AWHILE...DRINK PEOPLE NO ONE CARES ABOUT...

TEN LITTLE, NINE LITTLE, EIGHT LITTLE INDIANS! SEVEN LITTLE, SIX LITTLE, FIVE LITTLE INDIANS...♪

...FOUR LITTLE, THREE LITTLE, TWO LITTLE INDIANS...♪

LET'S TRY A CITY!

...ONE LITTLE♪ INDIAN BOY! ...URP!

TALK ABOUT POLITICALLY INCORRECT!

AN' YOU CAN'T SING, SKEETER, YOU SOUTHERN-FRIED WHITE-TRASH SLUT!

NOW THAT'S NOT TRUE A BIT! I HAVE A LOVELY VOICE AN' I'VE NEVER BEEN PREJUDICED WHEN IT COMES T' FEEDIN'!

EQUAL OPPORTUNITY, THAT'S MY MOTTO...

...THOUGH I DO PREFER BOYS!

GOT ANYWHERE IN MIND BESIDES WEST?

YEAH, I DO.

VEGAS.

LAS VEGAS, NEVADA. THAT'S WHERE HE WAS BORN AN' THAT'S WHERE THE BASTARDS TOOK HIM FROM ME.

PLEASE! CAN'T YOU JUST TELL ME WHERE HE IS?

I'M SORRY, MISS --THAT'S AGAINST EVERY RULE IN THE BOOK. HE'S A WARD OF THE STATE OF NEVADA, NOW.

BUT CAN'T YOU TELL ME SOMETHING... ANY-THING ABOUT WHAT'S HAPPENED TO HIM?

THAT'S WHEN I DIED THE FIRST TIME...

...BUT ONCE JUST WASN'T ENOUGH.

HEY NOW, SWEET THANG! WHEN I SAID I LIKED 'EM RELAXED, I DIDN'T MEAN DEAD!

THEM'S THE RULES! GET CLEAN OR GET OUT!

I DIDN'T KNOW THEY GREW THEIR WHORES SO MORAL IN NEVADA.

LISTEN, BABY GIRL, WE ARE LEGAL IN THIS STATE...

...AN' I CAIN'T AFFORD TO GET GUMMED UP WITH THE LAW ON ACCOUNT A' SOME BURNT-OUT TEEN-AGE JUNKIE!

I'M TWENTY-FOUR YEARS OLD!

THEN ACT YOUR DAMN AGE!

WHEN THE WORLD STOPS TURNING AND THE STARS BLINK OUT, I'LL STILL BE TWENTY-FOUR.

AN' DUMB AS DIRT, JENN. I'LL ALWAYS BE DUMB AS DIRT.

49

KIDS CAME OUT HERE T'NECK AN' TRIPPED OVER THE DANG THING! LOOKS LIKE YER TRUCKER, HANK. NOT A DROP LEFT IN HIM.

ED, OLE FRIEND... I BEEN THINKIN' 'BOUT RAISIN' MY FEE!

LOOKS LIKE YOUR CLIENT'S BROTHER-IN-LAW MIGHT JUSTA BEEN A RANDOM CASUALTY OF SOME PSYCHO CASE!

JUST A MINUTE, ED...

MISS?!

MISS, COULD I...?

KISS ME, COWBOY...

WAIT!

NEXT:
VIVA LAS VAMPS!

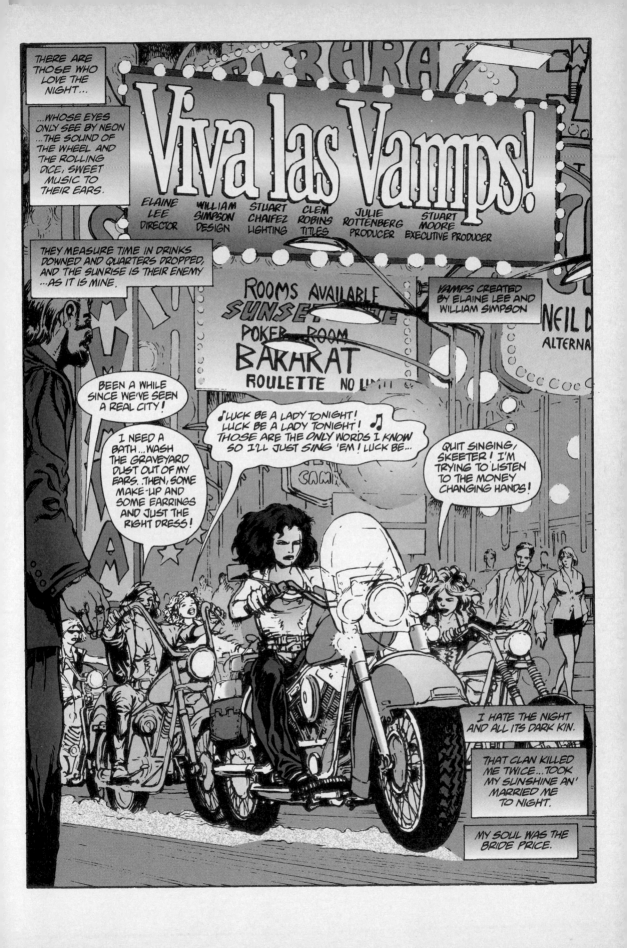

Viva las Vamps!

THERE ARE THOSE WHO LOVE THE NIGHT...

...WHOSE EYES ONLY SEE BY NEON ...THE SOUND OF THE WHEEL AND THE ROLLING DICE, SWEET MUSIC TO THEIR EARS.

ELAINE LEE
DIRECTOR

WILLIAM SIMPSON
DESIGN

STUART CHAIFEZ
LIGHTING

CLEM ROBINS
TITLES

JULIE ROTTENBERG
PRODUCER

STUART MOORE
EXECUTIVE PRODUCER

THEY MEASURE TIME IN DRINKS DOWNED AND QUARTERS DROPPED, AND THE SUNRISE IS THEIR ENEMY ...AS IT IS MINE.

VAMPS CREATED BY ELAINE LEE AND WILLIAM SIMPSON

ROOMS AVAILABLE
SUNSET
POKER ROOM
BAKARAT
ROULETTE NO LIMIT

NEIL D
ALTERNA

BEEN A WHILE SINCE WE'VE SEEN A REAL CITY!

I NEED A BATH...WASH THE GRAVEYARD DUST OUT OF MY EARS...THEN, SOME MAKE-UP AND SOME EARRINGS AND JUST THE RIGHT DRESS!

♪LUCK BE A LADY TONIGHT! LUCK BE A LADY TONIGHT! THOSE ARE THE ONLY WORDS I KNOW SO I'LL JUST SING 'EM! LUCK BE...

QUIT SINGING, SKEETER! I'M TRYING TO LISTEN TO THE MONEY CHANGING HANDS!

I HATE THE NIGHT AND ALL ITS DARK KIN.

THAT CLAN KILLED ME TWICE...TOOK MY SUNSHINE AN' MARRIED ME TO NIGHT.

MY SOUL WAS THE BRIDE PRICE.

THE DESERT END, ROOM 913...

WASN'T IT SWEET OF MY FRIEND TO BUY US THESE OUTFITS?

YOU SHOULDN'T HAVE *FINISHED* THE GUY, MINK...

...WE COULD'VE USED A MAKE-UP MIRROR. IT REALLY *BUMS* ME OUT THAT I CAN ONLY *SEE* MYSELF REFLECTED IN SOME *SOON-TO-BE DEAD* GUY'S EYEBALLS.

STOP TALKING, SKEETER.

I *HATE* IT THAT I CAN ONLY GO TO THE BEACH WHEN THE *MOON* IS OUT! AND COULD SOMEONE *PLEASE* HELP ME APPLY MY SUNTAN?

HEY, LOOK! LOOK AT THIS!

I'VE ALWAYS HEARD IT'S THE DRESS THAT MAKES THE WOMAN.

THE DRESS WILL *FADE*, MOMMI. BUT LOOK WHAT HAPPENS WHEN I SPRAY MY HAIR.

PSSSSSST!

I CAN ALMOST *SEE* MYSELF!

THAT'S *MARVELOUS*, SUGAR. NO ONE WOULD EVER KNOW THERE'S ANYTHING *ODD* ABOUT YA...

...EXCEPT, MAYBE, YOUR TASTE IN *DRESSES*. THEY CALL THAT COLOR HOOKER RED, DON'T THEY?

...AND YOU *THINK* THERE'S ANOTHER BODY OUT HERE?

YES...I *KNOW* THERE IS. I SAW IT IN A DREAM...JUST LIKE THE OTHER ONE...THE COWBOY.

AND THE TRUCKER THEY HIRED ME TO FIND.

I DIDN'T *SEE* YOUR TRUCKER, HANK, BUT THEY SAY HE WAS THE SAME...HIS BLOOD DRAINED AN' ALL.

ARE YOU ONE A'THOSE PSYCHICS, THEN? PARDON ME FOR SAYIN' THAT YOU LOOK A LITTLE *NORMAL* FOR THAT SORTA THING.

NO...NOT PSYCHIC. I'VE BEEN FOLLOWING DREAMS...VISIONS, REALLY...NOT *MY* VISIONS, BUT...OH, HELL!

MORE LIKE NIGHTMARES, IF YA ASK ME! AN' WHY'D YOU WANNA FOLLOW THAT KINDA DREAM? WHAT'S YER STAKE IN ALL THIS?

MY SISTER...I HAVEN'T SEEN HER IN YEARS...DIDN'T KNOW IF SHE WAS EVEN *ALIVE*, BUT...I THINK SHE *IS* BECAUSE I THINK I'M SEEING WHAT *SHE* SEES!

I WISH T'HECK I KNEW WHAT ALL THIS HAD T'DO WITH FIVE MISSIN' BIKERS AN' A MISSIN' CORPSE AN' A REFRIGERATOR TRUCK FULL OF MEAT. ALL I NEED'S A PSYCHIC WITH FAMILY PROBLEMS THROWN INTO TH' MIX!

AWWW JENNY...

WAIT!

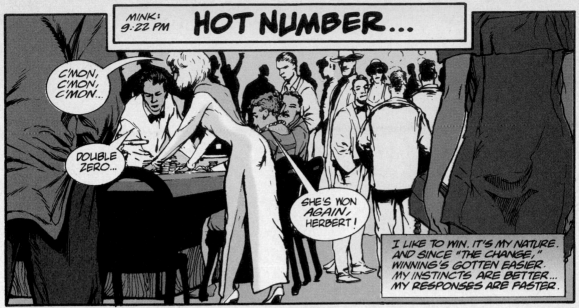

HOT NUMBER...

C'MON, C'MON, C'MON...

DOUBLE ZERO...

SHE'S WON *AGAIN*, HERBERT!

I LIKE TO WIN. IT'S MY NATURE. AND SINCE "THE CHANGE," WINNING'S GOTTEN EASIER. MY INSTINCTS ARE BETTER... MY RESPONSES ARE FASTER.

SOMETIMES I THINK IT SHOWS.

EXCUSE ME, MISS... YOU'RE SUCH A GOOD PLAYER... COULD YOU GIVE ME ANY ADVICE?

DON'T SPREAD YOUR CHIPS, DON'T PLAY CORNERS, PLAY THE ZEROES, AND, SWEETIE...

...DON'T EVER WEAR ANYTHING WITH HORIZONTAL STRIPES!

I LIKE BEING WHAT I AM... EXCEPT FOR LOSING MY TAN... AND ISN'T THAT WHAT IT'S ALL ABOUT? LIKING YOURSELF?

THAT, AND FEEDING. AFTER ALL, A GAL'S GOTTA EAT!

I'M OUT FOR NOW, CUTIE, BUT IF YOU'LL TELL ME WHEN YOU GET OFF WORK, WE COULD ARRANGE SOMETHING FOR LATER ...GO OUT FOR A BITE?

UH...I'M AFRAID THAT'S AGAINST THE RULES. I'M NOT SUPPOSED TO...

DIDN'T ANYONE TELL YOU, SWEETIE? RULES ARE MADE TO BE BROKEN...

ELEVEN SHARP.

A MAN IS LIKE A CABBAGE WITH A HANDLE. WHEN YOU NEED ONE, JUST GRAB THAT HANDLE AND PULL.

MERENGUE MOOLAH...

BACCARAT. THE GAME THAT SEPARATES MACHOS FROM MUCHACHOS.

TELL ME WHERE TO LAY MY MONEY, LADY LUCK.

WE'RE BETTING WITH THE BANK, POPPI.

THIS TIME, I GOT MYSELF A PLAYER.

THIS BET'S FOR THE BOYS.

AFTER YOU WIN THIS ONE, POPPI, YOU TAKE ME TO DINNER?

YOU BETCHA.

IN THE 1950's, THE GANGSTERS BROUGHT VEGAS-STYLE BACCARAT FROM CUBA, THE COUNTRY OF MY PARENTS, ACROSS TO THE STATES. HAVANA OR VEGAS...IN THOSE DAYS, THE GANGSTERS WERE THE SAME.

YOU'RE A NATURAL, BABY!

MAYBE THE GANGSTERS ARE ALWAYS THE SAME...ANYWHERE YOU GO. IT'S EASY TO SPOT THEM.

LEMME SETTLE UP MY COMMISSIONS.

THEY HAVE THE MONEY.

WHERE YOU WANNA GO, BABY?

SOMEPLACE THAT COSTS WAY TOO MUCH.

BACCARAT IS A VERY SIMPLE GAME, AND UNLIKE THE GAME OF LOVE, IT IS NOT SKILL THAT COUNTS, BUT SIZE. IF A MAN CANNOT AFFORD TO LOSE, HE IS TOO SMALL FOR BACCARAT, AND TOO SMALL FOR ME.

SCREECH: 9:45 PM **PORTRAIT OF THE ARTIST...**

THE SHARK GOES FISHING IN A SEA OF BOOZE.

I'M JUST INTERESTED.

IT'S EASY WORK, REALLY. THE MONEY'S GOOD AND THE CLIENTS ARE PRETTY WELL SCREENED...FOR GIRLS LIKE *US*, ANYWAY. ONCE IN A WHILE YOU GET A CREEP, BUT HEY...

...MOST WOMEN SLEEP WITH GUYS THEY DON'T WANT TO, FROM TIME TO TIME, AND ALL THEY GET'S A SALAD AND A SHOW. AM I RIGHT?

BEAUTIFUL TUNA. DRINKS SPRING WATER WITH A TWIST. ALCOHOL HURTS THE COMPLEXION ...HURTS THE POCKETBOOK. JUST GOOD BUSINESS.

I COULD SWIM IN YOU, PRETTY FISHY ...SWIM IN YOUR RED, RED SEA!

I WOULDN'T KNOW.

WELL, I *AM*. BUT TONIGHT I'VE GOT ONE I DON'T MIND...FROM CLEVELAND...SWEET GUY, JUST MARRIED TOO LONG...ALWAYS BRINGS ME *NICE* PRESENTS.

WELL...BETTER GO GET READY FOR HIM. LIKES EVERYTHING TO BE *ARRANGED* BEFORE HE GETS THERE. NICE CHATTING WITH YOU.

GOOD LUCK TO YOU, CINDY.

I THROW THE PRETTY FISHY BACK.

THERE ARE BIGGER CATCH IN THE OCEAN...

...AND TUNA'S GOOD FOR BAIT.

RM 123, 11:36

BLACKJACK SOUNDS LIKE SEX. THAT'S WHY I LIKE IT. DON'T THEY CALL THAT HAND A "DEALER'S STIFF"?

I'D CALL IT THAT...EVER SINCE YOU SAT DOWN TO PLAY!

SKEETER: 10 35 PM

DEVIL WITH A BLUE DRESS ON...

THAT...AND THE DEALERS ARE ALWAYS CUTE! ALL THE LADIES THINK SO...UNFORTUNATELY.

I'LL STAND.

ME, TOO.

WHAT ABOUT YOU, SOUTHERN GIRLZ? IF I "STAND" WILL YOU "SURRENDER"?

I'LL HAVE TO CONSIDER THAT PROPOSITION...

IT'S NOT THE BEST WAY TO WIN THE HAND, BUT I BEEN AROUND THE BLOCK ENOUGH T'KNOW...

I THINK I'LL DOUBLE DOWN.

...SPLIT YOUR TENS, AND THE QUEENS FOLLOW SUIT.

THAT'S IT.

THAT'S ALL FOR ME.

BLACKJACK PLAYERS ARE SUPERSTITIOUS...

...BUT I'D BET MY SWEET BOTTOM THAT THE DEALER ISN'T.

SO, SUGAR? HOW 'BOUT YOU AN' ME FINDIN' SOME PLACE THAT WE COULD DO SOME DOUBLIN' DOWN?

I WAS SICK OF THAT JOB, ANYWAY.

YOU'RE SO DECISIVE, SUGAR. I LOVE THAT IN A MAN.

SO HOW OLD ARE YOU? YOU LOOK TO BE A "SOFT SIXTEEN!"

I'M SOFT, AWRIGHT...BUT I WAS TWENTY ON MY LAST BIRTHDAY...

WELL THAT'S PERFECT, 'CAUSE I'M A "HARD TWENTY-SIX"!

MY GAMBLE PAYS OFF. THEY USUALLY DO. I BEEN ALIVE FOR TWENTY YEARS AN' DEAD FOR TWENTY MORE--AN' I KNOW A LI'L SOMETHIN' 'BOUT MEN!

62

LONE WOLF...

I'VE TRACKED THE MONSTER TO HIS DEN AND, FINDING HIM GONE, I ENTER.

THIS DEN SMELLS ROTTEN. IT'S FOULED WITH STOLEN BITS OF BROKEN LIVES...A POUND OF FLESH HERE, A SHREDDED HEART THERE...FOR THIS MONSTER IS A SCAVENGER.

HE FEEDS ON THE HARD-WON PAIN OF THE DESPERATE. HE STEALS AND THEN DEVOURS THEIR HOPE.

DARBY...DAVID... DAVIS...DAWSON... WHERE'S DAVISON, DAMMIT!

HE IS AN EVIL BEYOND ANY EVEN I HAVE KNOWN, AND TONIGHT, I SWEAR...

UGNH!

CRASH

...I'LL FEEL MY TEETH AROUND HIS COWARD'S THROAT!

WHAT I AM...

...IS...

JINGLE... CHINK... JING!

...RAGE.

SKWEEE

HEY, BABY, REMEMBER ME?

THERE'S SOMETHIN' I WANT FROM YOU...SOMETHIN' BESIDES MY POUND A' FLESH! BUT FIRST, A LITTLE DRINK...

...TO HELP YOU REMEMBER, BABY... REMEMBER WHAT I NEED TO KNOW!

MINK: 10:50 PM

HOT NUMBER...

DON'T BE SCARED, SWEETIE...

I DON'T REALLY MEAN THAT. I ENJOY HIS FEAR.

...YOU'D THINK YOU'D NEVER HAD A WOMAN BEFORE!

I HAVEN'T ...UH, I MEAN, YOU KNOW...NOT LIKE THIS!

AND HE'S GIVING ME GOBS OF ENJOYMENT!

IT'S NOT...I MEAN ...OF COURSE I WANT TO, IT'S JUST...I'M AFRAID I WON'T MEASURE UP TO YOUR EXPECTATIONS!

BUT THAT'S SILLY, SWEETIE. I REALLY, REALLY WANT YOU AND, I MEAN, WHADAYOO THINK'S GONNA HAPPEN THAT'S SO TERRIBLE, ANYWAY?

THIS IS EXACTLY THE KIND OF THING HE THOUGHT MIGHT HAPPEN.

YOU'RE JUST THE KINDA MAN I COULD SINK MY TEETH INTO!

NOW...IT HAS HAPPENED. HIS NUMBER'S UP.

SLAM

FEAR AND BLOOD AND BLOOD AND FEAR! GOOD ...GOOD...BETTER THAN SEX, SWEETIE...GOOD AS MONEY!

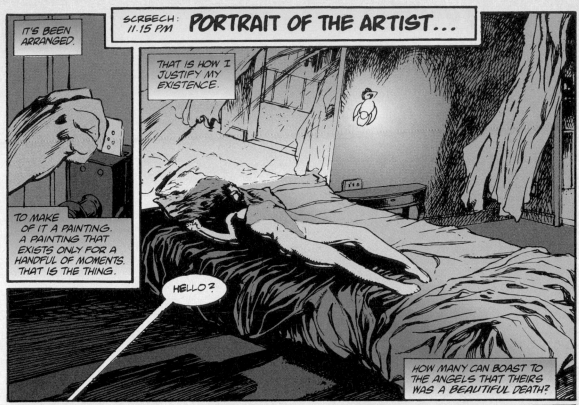

SCREECH: 11.15 PM **PORTRAIT OF THE ARTIST...**

IT'S BEEN ARRANGED.

THAT IS HOW I JUSTIFY MY EXISTENCE.

TO MAKE OF IT A PAINTING. A PAINTING THAT EXISTS ONLY FOR A HANDFUL OF MOMENTS. THAT IS THE THING.

HELLO?

HOW MANY CAN BOAST TO THE ANGELS THAT THEIRS WAS A BEAUTIFUL DEATH?

I'M HERE.

GREAT... GREAT...

THIS ONE WOULD HAVE DIED IN THE OFFICE...

...FACE DOWN ON HIS DESK...

REMOVE YOUR CLOTHING...

...A FAX OF THE MONTHLY SALES FIGURES PRESSED TO HIS OVERTAXED HEART.

SURE...SURE THING, GORGEOUS!

I WILL FREE HIM FROM THIS FATE.

I WILL MAKE HIS LIFE A POEM ...A SONG...

CINDY...

...A SONG OF BITTER LONGING...

WHAT? CINDY? WHAT ARE YOU... DEAD OR SOMETHING?

NOT DEAD, MY DARLING...

...MERELY DREAMING OF HEAVEN...

WHA...?!

ITS FINAL NOTE ...THE SWEETEST.

MY DANCE, BUT YOUR RHYTHM, LOVE...SWIM IN YOUR RED HEAT... DIVE IN IT...DROWN...

...SCREAM IT TO THE ANGELS, LOVE...

...TELL 'EM WE'VE KNOWN A BLISS BEYOND THE BEAUTY OF GOD'S FACE!

DEVIL WITH A BLUE DRESS...

LIKE MY MAMA USED T'SAY...IT'S BETTER WHEN THEY *LOVE* YA.

YOUR SKIN'S SO *COOL*!

WARM ME UP, BABY...

'COURSE, SHE WAS TALKIN' 'BOUT *S-E-X*!

...YEAH... THAT'S IT...WARM ME UP...

ALL THIS TIME AN' I STILL NEED THE *ACT*!

NEED THE *IDEA* OF IT.

I CAIN'T *STAND* T'THINK A' YOU BEIN' WITH ANYBODY ELSE.

OF LIFE HELD CAPTIVE 'TWIXT DEATH'S COLD THIGHS.

I'LL *NEVER* LEAVE YOU.

I KNOW...

SING TO ME, SUGAR! YEAH YEAH GIMME IT! SPEND THAT LIFE! LIFE IS HEAT! BURN ME WITH IT!

LITTLE DEATH, SUGAR PIE! NOW, GIMME THE REST...

...THE BIG DEATH. WHAT'S THAT SONG...THAT SONG... THAT SONG...

..."IT'S BEST TO LEAVE WHILE YOU'RE STILL IN LOVE."

THEY NEVER LEAVE ME, NOW.

THEY NEVER LEAVE.

WHERE WE GOIN' NOW, MOMMI?

NEW YORK.

HOLD THAT ELEVATOR!

THAS MY HOME TOWN, MOMMI. I'LL SHOW YOU A GOOD TIME.

C'MON, C'MON, C'MON!

HOT RUSH!

HEY! WAIT A MINUTE!

CAN'T. GOTTA HURRY.

HEY, MINK, WHAT DOES THE FLASHING RED LIGHT MEAN?

DING DING DING DING

TA·DA TA·DA TA·DA

LET GO OF ME, DAMMIT! THAT'S MY MONEY!

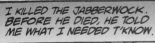

I KILLED THE JABBERWOCK. BEFORE HE DIED, HE TOLD ME WHAT I NEEDED T'KNOW.

I KNOW WHERE I'M GOIN' NOW.

THIS WAY!

I KNOW WHO I'M TRYIN' TO FIND.

BURY THE BIKES, BUT KEEP THE PLATES! STOW 'EM IN THE LUGGAGE!

THERE'S OTHER MONSTERS NEED SLAYIN', SEE?

MONSTERS WITH BIG CARS AN' OTHER PEOPLE'S HAPPINESS.

I'LL FIND THOSE MONSTERS...TRACK 'EM BY THE SMELL A' THEIR MONEY AN' GET 'EM WHERE THEY LIVE.

BRING THE HIGH ONES LOW...

THE AIRPORT, JAMES!

...AN' TAKE BACK WHAT IS MY OWN!

I'M PROBABLY GETTING MY "SUN TAN" ALL OVER THIS WHITE DRESS!

DEVIL WITH A BLUE DRESS ON!

ED SAYS THE CHEMICALS IN THE SKIN UNDER THE NAILS OF THAT TRUCK DRIVER WERE THE INGREDIENTS IN A POPULAR INSTANT SUNTAN PRODUCT.

WHO'D WANNA TAN A CORPSE? AND WHERE IS THE CORPSE, ANYWAY?

I DON'T KNOW, SWEET-HEART. I'M *BEGINNIN'* T'THINK IT GOT ON A MOTORCYCLE AN' RODE OFF.

GOODNESS, HANK! I NEARLY FORGOT T'TELL YA...

THEY FOUND ONE A' THOSE BIKERS YOU BEEN LOOKIN' FOR ...*DEAD*! BURIED OUT IN THE COUNTRY, UP IN CAROLINA. HUNTER WITH A DOG FOUND HIM. AN' GET THIS, GALLAGHER THERE WAS AN *EXTRA LEG* BURIED WITH 'IM!

HEY, GOOD-LOOKIN'! COME BACK T'SEE ME ALREADY?

WHAT!

DO I KNOW YOU?

SO WE'RE PLAYIN' IT THAT WAY, ARE WE? YES, YOU *KNOW* ME! YOU WERE IN HERE JUST THE OTHER NIGHT, SITTIN' OVER YONDER, AN' IF YOU DON'T THINK YOU KNOW ME, YOU C'N GIMME MY BOOK BACK!

HECK, JUDY! RECKON THIS MEANS I'M LOOKIN' FOR THREE AN' A HALF BIKERS?

I'M SORRY...YOU MUST'VE MISTAKEN ME FOR SOMEONE... YOU MUST'VE...

WHAT?!--

NO, NO, NO, **NO!**

JEEZUZ H!

JENNY!

AIIE! A VISION! ANOTHER VISION!

NONONONO! NOT THE SUN! BURNING! KILLING ME! KILLING US!

NOW, THE SUN SETS EARLIER IN NEW YORK THAN IT DOES IN VEGAS BY...TWO...OR MAYBE THREE HOURS? SO IF IT'S ONE O'CLOCK NOW, AN' IT TAKES FIVE HOURS TO GET THERE, SUBTRACTING THE HOUR WE'VE FLOWN ALREADY AND AT LEAST TWO HOURS FOR THE TIME CHANGE...THAT WOULD BE...THREE... FOUR...FIVE A.M.? THAT'S *WELL* BEFORE SUNRISE? WHEN DID YOU SAY SUNRISE WAS AGAIN?

uh-uh, SKEETER, I DON'T THINK THAT'S...

WE HURTLE TOWARD MORNING IN A SKIN OF AIRBORNE METAL. SUDDENLY I FEEL HER WITH ME!

JENNY, MY TWIN. HER HUMAN MIND TAKES HOLD OF ME. I SEE WHAT SHE SEES. KNOW WHAT SHE KNOWS.

AND OUR UNDEAD SOUL IS IMMOLATED ON A PYRE OF OUR OWN FLESH.

JENNY! NO!

THE SKY EXPLODES WITH BLINDING HEAT...

WE ARE CONSUMED BY LIGHT!

NEXT: **INTO THE SUNRISE!**

76

PUH-DUHM! PUH-DUHM!

MY FANGS SINK INTO THE MAN'S DEFENSELESS THROAT AND HIS BLOOD, SALT AND HOT, FLOODS INTO ME. EASY, BABY, EASY...WANNA GO GO GO, BUT GOTTA TAKE IT SLOW ...SLOW AN' EASY...

...DRINK TOO MUCH, WE'LL DROP LIKE A BOMB, INTO THE GARDEN STATE'S HEART!

PUH-DUHM! PUH-DUHM!

PUH-DUHM! PUH-DUHM! PUH-

...HEART...HEART...PUMP IT, BABY! GIMME THAT STUFF! THAT'S IT, BABY! FLY ME TO THE MOON AND BACK!

HOWLER! HURRY UP, MOMMI! I NEED SOME HELP!

GEEZE LOUISE. NEARLY GOT LOST...I COULDA KILLED THE GUY!

NEVER MIND, MOMMI. I'LL GET THE BAGS. YOU TOO BLOOD-DRUNK TO HELP ANYBODY.

VISION FUNNY...BLOOD, SWEET BLOOD...MAKIN' MY BELLY WARM AN' KNEES...WOBBLY...PULL IT TOGETHER NOW...THINK...GOTTA THINK...

WE'RE BEGINNING OUR DESCENT, SO PLEASE KEEP YOUR SEAT BELTS FASTENED AND REMAIN IN YOUR SEATS UNTIL WE ARRIVE AT THE GATE.

OH...AND PAY NO ATTENTION TO THAT SOUND OF RIPPING METAL.

MMMMMMMM!

NEVER FLOWN FIRST CLASS BEFORE. MY PALS SEEM TO LIKE THE COMPLIMENTARY DRINKS.

THEN, WITH THE EARTH'S BLOOD PULSING WE'T AROUND US, WE SWIM EAST, TOWARD THE CITY...

...ITS BUILDINGS, LONG AND BLACK AGAINST THE PALE HORIZON, WARN OF THE COMING LIGHT.

WHERE WE GON' FIND A CEMETERY IN NEW YORK?

TRUST ME, MOMMI.

TRUST DON'T COME EASY FOR CREATURES LIKE US...

AS FAR AS I CAN THROW YA, HONEY.

NOT FOR VAMPIRES... NOT FOR WOMEN.

THERE! GRANT'S TOMB!

YOU 'SPECT ME T'SLEEP WITH A DRUNKEN YANKEE?

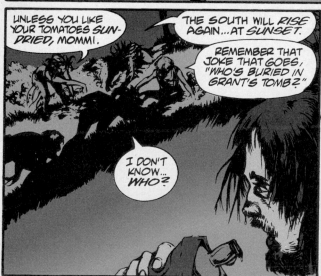

UNLESS YOU LIKE YOUR TOMATOES SUN-DRIED, MOMMI.

THE SOUTH WILL RISE AGAIN...AT SUNSET.

REMEMBER THAT JOKE THAT GOES, "WHO'S BURIED IN GRANT'S TOMB?"

I DON'T KNOW... WHO?

US, MINK... WE ARE!

OH.

TRUST...SOMETIMES GIVEN FREELY, SOMETIMES EARNED. FOR US, IT'S IN THE BLOOD-BOND...IN THE WAY THE PACK DECOYS THE WITLESS PREY. COME SUNRISE, WE TAKE IT WITH US TO THE GRAVE.

SO THERE WERE *FOUR* MURDERS AT THE HOTEL NIGHT-BEFORE LAST...TWO GUESTS, AND TWO EMPLOYEES OF THE CASINO! AND, YOU THINK YOU MIGHT HAVE SOMETHING ON TAPE?

WELL, HANK, LIKE I TOLD THE COPS LAST NIGHT...THE SECURITY CAMERAS ARE MOUNTED RIGHT BENEATH THIS WINDOW...YOU CAN SEE THE WHOLE FLOOR FROM HERE. NOW, TAKE A LOOK AT THE FIRST MONITOR...

...THERE'S THE DEALER...THE ONE THEY FOUND DEAD IN THE SECOND-FLOOR ROOM? JUST WALKED AWAY FROM HIS TABLE. NOTICE ANYTHING FUNNY? LOOK CLOSE. THE GUY'S *TALKIN'* ...TALKIN' TO *NOBODY!*

NOW, LEMME RUN THIS *BACK* A BIT...

PLAY

...THERE! SEE THAT? THIS IS JUST A LITTLE EARLIER. THE GUY'S DEALIN' CARDS TO *THREE* PLAYERS, BUT THERE'S ONLY *TWO* AT THE TABLE. *WEIRD,* AM I RIGHT?

AN' HE'S THE ONE THEY FOUND IN 'IZ BIRTHDAY SUIT...JUST FINISHED SOME FANCY WRES-TLIN' WITH A PERSON A' THE OPPOSITE GENDER?

MADE TIME WITH THE INVISIBLE WOMAN AND LIVED TO *REGRET* IT, IF YA ASK ME!

USE YOUR PHONE?

≥YAWN≥ SORRY... COULDN'T SLEEP LAST NIGHT.

DON'T THINK *MANY* PEOPLE SLEPT WELL LAST NIGHT. COPS WERE TELLIN' ME ABOUT ANOTHER *MURDER.* SOMEBODY BROKE INTO OLD JUDGE BAKER'S HOUSE AND KILLED HIM. *ANOTHER WEIRD ONE.*

WHADAYA MEAN, "WEIRD"?

MR. BEDGOOD? HANK GALLAGHER...

WHAT I MEAN IS *FINGER-PRINTS* WERE *FOUND...*PRINTS BELONGING TO A WOMAN'S BEEN *DEAD THREE YEARS!*

LISTEN, MR. BEDGOOD... I HAVEN'T FOUND TH'PERSON THAT KILLED YOUR BROTHER-IN-LAW YET, BUT I THINK I NEED TA TELL YA, WE'RE INTA SOMETHIN' *VERY WEIRD* HERE. I'M BEGINNIN' TA THINK WE'RE DEALIN' WITH SOME KINDA GHOSTS OR *VAMPIRES* OR SOMETHIN'.

WHAT?! ARE YOU *CRAZY* OR ...OH! heh heh! YOU HAD ME GOIN' THERE FOR A MINUTE, GALLAGHER! I THOUGHT YOU WAS ON TH' *LEVEL!*

THE PRINTS WERE ALL OVER SOME OF THE JUDGE'S OLD FILES... FILES TO DO WITH SOME *HOOKER'S* BABY THAT WAS TAKEN BY THE COURT, AND THEN SENT TO SOME NEW YORK *LAWYER* WHO HAD CLIENTS WAITING TO *ADOPT.*

DEAD DEALER-COP

BUT LISTEN, WHILE I GOTCHA ON TH' *PHONE...*SOME GUY AN' 'IS HUNTIN' DAWG FOUND THE BODIES A' THOSE BIKERS YOU BEEN CHASIN'; BURIED IN TH' WOODS, SO I GUESS THEY AIN'T *THEM!* AN' YOU WAS WRONG ABOUT SOMETHIN' ELSE... THERE WERE SIX OF 'EM, NOT FIVE!

SIX?!

AND GET THIS...

YEAH, I SAID SIX! AN' ONE SLIMBITCH WAS CUT TO PIECES, AN' A PIECE OF 'IM WAS THROWN INTA TH' GRAVES WITH EACH A' THE FIVE OTHER SUMBITCHES!

GEEZE-AWMIGHTY-CHRISTOPHER!

...THEY RUN A MAKE ON THE PRINTS? WHAT COMES UP? THE *HOOKER!* THE WOMAN *DIED* OF AN OVER-DOSE, NOT LONG AFTER THEY TOOK THE KID? AND *THREE YEARS LATER,* HER PRINTS ARE ALL OVER THE CASE FILES, AND THE JUDGE WHO TOOK THE KID LYIN' DEAD *BESIDE* 'EM!

NO NO NO ...HANK!

WE HAVE TO GO TO NEW YORK.

WE RISE AT SUNSET, HAVING SLEPT A BRUTAL DAY BENEATH THE CITY THAT *NEVER SLEEPS*.

MUCH OBLIGED, GENERAL...BUT WE REALLY HAVE TO BE GOIN' NOW.

THE GROUND ROARS HERE...GROANS WITH TURBINES, TRAINS, AND TRAFFIC... BELCHES STEAM AND GRIT. ENOUGH TO WAKE THE DEAD.

WELL, "HEY" TO YOU, TOO!

GEE! WHAT'S A GIRL HAFTA DO TO GET A REACTION AROUND HERE?

IN NEW YORK WE'RE JUST ONE OF THE CROWD, MOMMI.

HEY! I KNOW WHAT YOU ARE...

YE'R THE DEVIL GIRLS...THE DEVIL GIRLS! WHEN BAD GIRLS DIE, THE MAN IN HELL TAKES THEIR CAST-OFF SKINS AND STUFFS 'EM WITH EVIL...MAKES NEW DEVILS WITH 'EM TO TORMENT THE EARTH! YER SKINS ARE STUFFED WITH DEATH!

YE'R DEVIL GIRLS!

WELL, MR. SCREWLOOSE ...I KNOW WHAT YOU ARE TOO...

...YOU'RE DEAD!

EVEN IN TIMES OF LITTLE FAITH, THERE ARE THOSE WHO BELIEVE...

...AND THE SIGNS AND *SYMBOLS* OF FAITH ARE WEAPONS THAT CAN BE USED *AGAINST* US.

A CROSS IS JUST ONE. THERE ARE OTHERS.

BACK, YOU FEMALE DEVIL!

SOMEHOW, ALONG THAT DARK PATH BETWEEN THE SHATTERED SYNAPSE AND THE MISFIRED NEURON, THE MAN HAD FOUND FAITH.

YOU CAN'T TOUCH ME! I GOT THE POWER! I GOT THE SHIELD A' CERTAIN GOODNESS! MAN GIMME IT! MAN WITH THE TWO-TONE HEAD!

HIS SYMBOL IS AS GOOD AS ANY.

WHAT KIND OF NEIGHBORHOOD IS THIS, ANYWAY? LOOKS DANGEROUS.

YOU WORRIED 'BOUT MUGGERS, MINK?

DANGEROUS FOR THE LIVING, MAYBE.

AN' DON'T COME BACK!

MAYBE DANGEROUS FOR US, TOO! TOO MANY ADDICTS AND AIDS VICTIMS HERE. WE'LL GO EAST SIDE...THROUGH THE PARK!

START SPREADIN' THE NOOZ! ♪ RED BLOOD IS MY BOOZE! I WANNA DRINK A PART OF IT, OF OLE NOO YAWK! ♪

EAST, THROUGH HARLEM, TO THE TOP OF CENTRAL PARK. I'LL RUN WITH THE PACK 'TIL WE FIND MEAT AND TRANSPORT, THEN PEEL OFF T'DO SOME HUNTIN' ON MY OWN!

GOT ME A MONSTER TO TRACK...

...ANOTHER MONSTER. IT'S EASY AS PIE T'FIND 'EM. JUST LOCATE THE ALPHA MONSTER, AN' FOLLOW THE TRAIL OF SHIT.

WHERE IS HE? WHERE'S MY BOY?

I DON'T KNOW! I SWEAR DON'T...

AT THE END OF THE SHIT TRAIL, THERE'S ALWAYS ANOTHER MONSTER.

FIELDS...ROBERT FIELDS...ATTORNEY FROM NEW YORK...SAID THERE WAS MONEY IN IT...HAD CLIENTS WITH BIG MONEY...NICE FOLKS ...BABIES BETTER OFF...

THANKS...

...NOW DIE!

THEY ALL LEAVE THESE TRAILS...MARK THEIR TERRITORY. I CAUGHT THE SCENT IN VEGAS, AN' FOLLOWED THE DROPPINS CLEAR TO NEW YORK.

CENTRAL PARK.

I THINK I SEE SOME-THING COMING.

OH GOODIE... A LIMOUSINE!

OH MY GOD!

AIIIIHHHH!

RELA-A-AX, SWEETIE. YOU'LL HARDLY FEEL A THING.

PUH-DUHM! PUH-DUHM! PUH-DUHM!

IT'S STARTED...THAT OLE DRUM'S BEAT-BEAT-BEAT ...KEEPS US DANCIN'...

WE GOT ON OUR BLOOD-RED DANCIN' SHOES AN' WE CAN'T STOP IT NOW! CAN'T STOP THE DANCE!

LOOKS LIKE THE EAST SIDE COMES TO US, MOMMI.

PUH-DUHM! PUH-DUHM!

NOW, WAIT A MINUTE! YOU CAN'T JUST...

SURE WE CAN, HONEY.

LOVE THE OUTFIT. THE PEARLS ARE A NICE TOUCH.

PEARLS OF THE ORIENT...

PUH-DUHM!

MIGHT AS WELL TRY TO STOP THE MOVE-MENT OF THE EARTH, OR THE CRASH OF THE BREAK-ING WAVE.

PUH-DUHM! PUH-DUHM!

WAVE AFTER WAVE AFTER...RICH BLOOD ...MONEY BLOOD...BLUE, BLUE, BLUE, RED SALT SEA WASHING THE DEATH AWAY...

JUST A LITTLE BIT, HONEY. DON'T DRAIN 'IM. WE NEED 'IM TO SIGN THE CHECK.

...MMMM...FIRE WATER...BREAK THROUGH ME...WASH AWAY MY SINS...THAT'S IT THAT'S IT THAT'S--

HOWLER!

WHATZ!

DAMN! NIPPED IN THE BLOOD!

WE'RE HERE, MOMMI.

THROUGH THE PINK-HOT HAZE THAT BLANKETS A VAMP WHEN SHE FEEDS, THE NEON SIGN BURNS LIKE A MORNING SUN. TIME TO RIDE!

HARLE

DANG IT, HOWLER! YOU NEARLY KILLED THAT GUY AN' YOU NEARLY KILLED ME...AGAIN! I DON'T SEE WHY WE CAN'T JUST ALL FEED AT ONCE? IT'S TOO PAINFUL T'HOLD OFF WHILE EVER'BODY ELSE IS EATIN'!

TOO DANGEROUS...ALL OF US BLOOD-DRUNK AT ONCE... DAVE...ASK DAVE!

DAVE IS UNDER TH' GROUND IN FIVE DIFFERENT GRAVES, MOMMI...AND A STAKE IN HIS BASTARD HEART!

TRUE...TOO TRUE...DAVE'S DEAD. WE KILLED HIM. NOW TO GET THE RIDES ...GET THE RIDES AND GO HUNTIN' MONSTERS.

NOTHIN' LIKE CHOOSIN' A SPANKIN' NEW SCOOT, TO SOBER A GAL UP.

NOW, YOU CAN'T JUST RIDE 'EM OUTTA THE SHOP WITH NO PLATES.

WE GOT PLATES, POPPI. WE BROUGHT 'EM WITH US.

OKAY, THEN. SURE YOU WON'T CHANGE YOUR MIND ABOUT THAT DATE, GORGEOUS?

WE GOT A PACT, SWEETIE. WE NEVER GO OUT WITH BIKERS OR BIKE DEALERS.

THAT HARDLY SEEMS FAIR!

NOT FAIR, MAYBE, BUT LUCKY FOR YOU.

I BELIEVE...THIS WILL BE SUFFICIENT...TO COVER THE COST OF THESE MOTORCYCLES...

CASH IT FAST, HONEY. IT'S HARD T'TELL WHEN A SUGAR DADDY MIGHT WAKE UP AN' SEE TH' ERROR OF HIS WAYS!

LET'S GET GOIN', LADIES. THE NIGHT'S NOT GETTING ANY YOUNGER...

AND A COLD, BLUE SIP OF SOCIALITE'S BLOOD IS HARDLY ENOUGH TO LAST ME 'TIL DAWN.

THROUGH THE STREETS OF THE CITY, WE ROAR...THE NEW ANGELS...BORN NOT FROM A LIVING HELL, BUT FROM THE DEAD SILENCE OF THE GRAVE.

I'LL DRINK MANHATTAN, THE BRONX AND STATEN ISLAND TOO! ♪

ONE GOOD THING ABOUT THE TRAFFIC...YOU CAN'T HEAR SKEETER SING!

TONIGHT...
KABLAMACHUNK!

TIME FOR ALL GOOD VAMPS TO DANCE TO A DIFFERENT BEAT...TRADE IN THE RED SHOES FOR A PAIR IN BLUE SUEDE.

YOU'RE EVIL, SKEETER!

WHY YOU GOTTA CHOOSE ONE THAT PLAYS MUSIC LIKE THAT? YOU DRINK HIM, YOU KILL THE MUSIC.

I DON'T CHOOSE 'EM, HONEY. THEY CHOOSE ME!

AND HE'S THE ONE. BESIDES...

...YOU KNOW THERE'S MORE TO IT THAN JUST WHIPPIN' UP LUNCH!

I'M TRYING TO LOCATE A MR. ROBERT FIELDS... HE'S AN ATTORNEY...HE'S ...YES, I'LL WAIT.

I'M NOT A GOOD VAMP. I HAVE A SECRET. WHILE THE GALS STALK DINNER ON THE DANCE FLOOR, I'M TRACKIN' GREED DOWN A FIBER OPTIC TRAIL.

YES... I'LL WAIT... I'VE GOT ALL NIGHT.

THE MUSIC'S BLOOD-HOT. IT MOANS AND THROBS, RIDING MY VAMPIRE SENSES, FILLS ME LIKE THE SOUND OF A THOUSAND HAMMERING HEARTS. BUT I DON'T LET IT CARRY ME... TAKE ME AWAY. I AM A COLD BITCH WITH A MISSION AND A POCKETFUL OF CHANGE.

WILSON COUNTY MORGUE, NORTH CAROLINA.

I DUNNO WHAT YOU GOT TA SMILE ABOUT, BUDDY... BUT AFTER WE GET RID A' THIS STICK IN YOUR CHEST, WE'LL TAKE A LOOK AN' FIND OUT.

OH NO. OH GOD, NO. NOT NOW. NOT DAVE.

PUH-DUHM PUH-DUHM PUH-DA-DUHM PA DA DA DA

AGGGHHHHH NO! HH!

AIIIIIIIIIIIIIIIII!

OH LOOK, A LEG-- AND GIFTWRAPPED!

THANKS, DAVE! LET ME DOWN THIS, AND WE'LL DANCE.

NAME'S DON. WHO'S DAVE?

I KNOW YOU'RE BACK, YOU BASTARD. BUT, I'M ALMOST HOME... ALMOST...

THIS A CHILD-PROOF PACKAGE, DOC?

C'MON...

DAVE...IT'S DAVE! HE'S BACK! I CAN FEEL HIM!

I KNOW, MOMMI. I FEEL HIM, TOO.

KEEP LOCKED

MINK! SKEETER!

SKEETER! WE KNOW YOU'RE HERE, MOMMI. GET YOUR TEETH OUTTA THAT BOY AN' YOUR TAIL IN GEAR!

RAGGHHH!

GODDANG IT! YOU STOLE MY PEAK! I WAS ALMOST...

WE GOT WORSE THINGS TO WORRY ABOUT, SKEETER. DAVE'S BACK!

SO, GET YOUR DRUNKEN SELF TOGETHER, 'CAUSE IF THAT BASTARD FINDS US, WE'LL BE WISHING WE WERE REALLY DEAD.

MINK! WE GOTTA MAKE PLANS. DAVE'S...

YEAH, I KNOW. I FELT IT. WHERE'S HOWLER?

I SAW HER LEAVE THE CLUB. THAT WAS SOME TIME AGO. DON'T KNOW WHERE SHE WENT...

"TO MARKET TO MARKET TO BUY A FAT PIG..."

...BUT I GOT A BETTER QUESTION. WHERE'S DAVE?

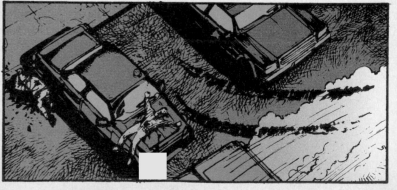

97

MONEY...THAT'S WHAT IT WAS ALL ABOUT. THAT'S WHY THEY TOOK YOU, MY LOVE...

...WHY THEY CRACKED MY HEART AN' TORE ALL THE GOODNESS OUT...

NO ONE AROUND.

...WHY THEY STOLE THE SUN FROM ME!

AGHHH!

THEY'LL PAY FOR IT, NOW...

...THEY'LL PAY.

NICE PLACE. IT *SHOULD* BE... BOUGHT, AS IT WAS, WITH BUSTED LIVES AN' MAMAS' TEARS.

YOU? ARE *YOU* THE ONE? YES... THERE HE IS...THE END OF ONE TRAIL, THE START OF ANOTHER.

JUST FOLLOW THE SHIT.

WHA... WHO?!

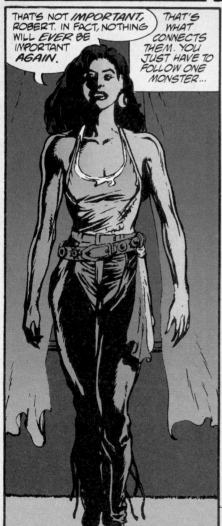

THAT'S NOT *IMPORTANT*, ROBERT. IN FACT, NOTHING WILL *EVER* BE IMPORTANT *AGAIN*.

THAT'S WHAT CONNECTS THEM. YOU JUST HAVE TO FOLLOW ONE MONSTER...

...TO ANOTHER.

NOW, I'M JUST GONNA CRAWL IN BED WITH YOU AND LET YOU TELL ME *EVERYTHING* YOU KNOW...

NEXT:
THE POISON APPLE

WELCOME TO **DELAWARE**

I'M AS HUNGRY AS A COYOTE IN A CONDO, AND NOT A LAP DOG IN SIGHT! BUT, OLE DAVE'S GOT NO TIME FOR HUNTING TONIGHT...

...NOT TILL I *FIND* THOSE BITCHES THAT *BURIED* ME!

FIND 'EM AND *BURN* 'EM!

OH, LOOK! ROAD FOOD!

I'LL JUST DO THE DRIVE-THRU!

KER*RASH*

HOLD THE PICKLES!

HA HA HA HA HA HA HA HA

PUH-DUHM! PUH-DUHM! PUH-DUH...!

102

THIS WAY!

MY NEIGHBORHOOD... BY NAME, WASHINGTON HEIGHTS... BY PRECINCT, THIRTY-TWO. WE GOT MORE MURDERS HERE THAN ANYPLACE ELSE IN THE WHOLE CIUDAD.

YOU DON' WANNA BE STOPPING HERE AT NIGHT. NOT UNLESS YOU LOOK THE PART, WALK THE WALK AND TALK THE TALK.

WHERE THE HELL ARE WE?

IT IS A PLACE WHERE STOLEN CARS ARE TAKEN, STRIPPED, IGNITED... THE YOUNG THIEVES SOMETIMES COOKING HOT DOGS OVER THE AUTO'S FUNERAL PYRE. THEY DRINK BEER. THEY SMOKE THEIR CRACK. FOR THEM, IT IS A PICNIC.

TONIGHT A TOYOTA BURNS. THE BANDIDO'S CHOICE! WITH PARTS VERY EASY TO SELL, SO THAT DRUGS CAN BE BOUGHT.

WHY'RE WE STOPPING?

YEAH! LET'S GET GOING. DAVE'S PROBABLY IN JERSEY BY NOW!

I KNOW SOMEONE WHO CAN HELP US. SOMEONE NEARBY.

THE ONLY THING THAT CAN HELP US IS DISTANCE...

IT IS HOWLER WHO SPEAKS FROM THE SHADOWS. SHE HAS FELT MY INTENTION, AND COME TO THIS PLACE.

THIS IS HOW IT IS WITH US. WE KNOW THINGS.

WE FEEL.

...I SAY WE HEAD NORTH. AWAY.. AWAY FROM DAVE.

BUT I DO NOT FEEL HER NOW. SHE PULLS BACK FROM US. HIDES.

NO, MOMMI, IT'S NO GOOD. HE WILL FIND US ANYWHERE WE RUN. BESIDES...

...YOU BEEN ACTING TOO CRAZY. DISAPPEARING. TAKING US PLACES, WE DON' KNOW WHY. WE COULD BE IN SAN DIEGO, MOMMI, OR IN MEXICO. YOU TELL US TO GO TO THE SAME DAMN COAST AS THAT CRAZY SUNUFFA BITCH.

YEAH, SUGAR...YOU NEARLY GOT US SUN-BURNT, FLYIN' EAST ON THAT PLANE!

SHE'S BEHAVING ALMOST...HUMAN.

LISTEN HERE. I SAID WE'RE GOIN' NORTH, AN' WE... ARE ...GOIN'...

...NORTH!

WHACK!

UGHN!

NORTH.

HOWLER, ARE YOU NUTS?

WE'RE GOING NORTH.

SEEING RED. STOLEN BLOOD SEETHING IN DEATH-COLD VEINS ...IT BOILS...STEAMS...TO RISE LIKE A RED MIST, CLOUDING THE ANGRY EYE.

YOU RIPPED MY GOOD JACKET, MOMMI.

NOW, LIKE A CAT, I SEE ONLY THE ENEMY'S MOVEMENT...

...SEE THE STREAK OF RED/IT/HER... ALL HOT VERMILLION MOTION...FAST HEAT!

WE ARE ANIMAL...

I KILL YOU AGAIN!

ONE ANIMAL, THE FIVE OF US. I AM THE HEAD NOW...SHE IS THE LEG THAT IS CAUGHT IN THE TRAP. SO THAT SHE WILL NOT KILL US, I GNAW HER OFF!

FIGHT!

107

...PRETTY PLEASE!

WAIT, SKEETER...!

...WE GOT TROUBLE.

OH, SHOOT! MORE OF 'EM.

I DISAGREE, SCREECH. THIS DOESN'T LOOK LIKE TROUBLE TO ME...

...IT LOOKS LIKE LUNCH!

NO, MINK! WAIT...

...WE LEAVE A BIG PILE OF BODIES DOWN HERE, SOMEONE'S GONNA THINK THAT'S STRANGE AN' WANNA LOOK INTO IT.

WHO'S GONNA NOTICE A FEW MORE BODIES IN NEW YORK?

HE'LL NOTICE, MINK! DAVE'LL NOTICE!

SHE'S RIGHT. DON'T KILL THEM, JUST...

...HURT THEM A LITTLE!

'COURSE, DAVE CAN FIND US WITHOUT NO BODIES. I JUST DON' WANNA BRING HIM HERE, TO THE HEIGHTS, NOT HERE...NOT AGAIN.

FOLLOW ME! UPSTAIRS!

KISSES!

MACHISMO IS WHAT WE COUNT ON. DEAD BODIES WOULD TALK, BUT THESE MUCHACHOS WON'T. WHAT WOULD THEY SAY?

THEY KNOW THE COPS DON' GIVE A RAT'S ASS.

WHAT DO COPS CARE IF SOME NIÑAS BREAK THE BALLS OF A COUPLA CAR THIEF PUNKS?

ARE YOU READY TO LEAVE WITH ME NOW?

NO. NO MORE RUNNING, MOMMI. WE STAY...AND WE FIND A WAY TO GET RID OF DAVE. FOR GOOD.

BELIEVE. IT OR NOT.

YEAH, SWEETIE.

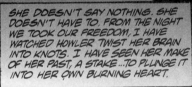

OKAY. THAT'S THAT.

YOU'RE ALL WITH HER?

YES, WE ARE.

SHE DOESN'T SAY NOTHING. SHE DOESN'T HAVE TO. FROM THE NIGHT WE TOOK OUR FREEDOM, I HAVE WATCHED HOWLER TWIST HER BRAIN INTO KNOTS. I HAVE SEEN HER MAKE OF HER PAST, A STAKE...TO PLUNGE IT INTO HER OWN BURNING HEART.

I HAVE FELT THE GREAT TEETH COMING DOWN ON HER.

THE TEETH OF THE TRAP BITE INTO HER SOFT MEAT AND THE PAIN MAKES HER CRAZY. LOCO IN LA CABEZA!

WHO BAITS THE TRAP? WHO SETS IT? I DON' KNOW. BUT I FEEL ITS TEETH IN HER. AND LIKE A LEG THAT HAS BEEN CUT OFF FROM THE BODY, I WILL STILL FEEL HER PAIN, WHEN SHE HAS GONE.

THIS IS IT...THE HOUSE IN MY DREAM. THIS IS WHERE I SAW HER.

YES. I SAW THE NUMBER. AND THERE WAS A BABY...NO... A *WOLF*, A BABY WOLF, LOOKING OUT THE WINDOW.

JENN? IF WE *FIND* YOUR SISTER...?

SLAM

YOU'RE SURE ABOUT THAT, JENNY?

HANK GALLAGHER?

THAT'S ME. GLAD T' SEE YA, DETECTIVE.

YEAH, WELL, YOUR STORY CHECKED OUT.

THE BOYS DOWN IN TEXAS SAID YOU SEEMED TO BE ONTO SOMETHIN', AN' THAT YOUR PSYCHIC FRIEND HAD TURNED UP A BODY IN NEW MEXICO.

THAT SHE DID, SIR. AN' NOW WE THINK OUR PERPETRATOR'S MADE A VISIT TO THE FOLKS LIVIN' IN THIS HOUSE.

BAM BAM BAM BAM

I'LL BE HONEST WITH YOU TWO...

...I DON'T PUT MUCH STOCK IN THIS AMAZING KRESKIN KIND OF STUFF.

YES... WHO IS IT?

DETECTIVE CAVALARO, NYPD. WE NEED TO TALK TO YOU, MA'AM.

WHAT'S WRONG, OFFICER? THERE HASN'T BEEN A ROBBERY IN THE NEIGHBORHOOD?

DETECTIVE, MA'AM...AND I'LL EXPLAIN EVERYTHING TO YOU. BUT FIRST, MAYBE YOU COULD GET YOUR HUSBAND FOR US?

OH... CERTAINLY...

...BUT GIVE ME A MINUTE. HE'S IMPOSSIBLE TO WAKE UP. BOBBY COULD SLEEP THROUGH A NUCLEAR WAR... I ALWAYS SAY IT'S LIKE WAKING THE DEAD.

TAKE YOUR TIME, MRS. FIELDS.

REMINDS ME...I DID A LITTLE CHECKING UP. THIS GUY ROBERT FIELDS IS A LAWYER...BIG LEAGUE ...KNOWN FOR ARRANGING ADOPTIONS...

EEEEE

NO! NO! NOOOOOO!

GEEZE!

OH, NO...

LOOKS LIKE YOU WERE RIGHT.

HERE...LET ME HELP YOU...

I WAS IN BED WITH HIM? I WAS SLEEPING WITH HIM? WHAT...? HOW...?

NO PULSE...DAMN! SKIN'S COLD.

WEIRD WOUND. BETTER CALL THIS IN.

I THOUGHT HE WAS ASLEEP...SLEEPS LIKE THE DEAD...BOBBY ...WHO WOULD HURT BOBBY? HE HELPS PEOPLE...GIVES THEM JOY...

C'MON...C'MON...ANSWER THE PHONE, WILLYA! GUESS THIS'LL TEACH ME TO BE A GODDAMN SKEPTIC! RIGHT, GALLAGHER?

GALLAGHER...?

...GOTCHA!

BABY BOY ROSS... ADDRESS IN UPSTATE NEW YORK. WELL, BABY BOY... I'D BE WILLIN' T' BET YOU GOT A LOT IN COMMON WITH BABY BOY DAVISON, AN' I BET YOUR MAMA KNOWS THAT, TOO!

NEVADA/BABY BOY ROSS

113

SEVEN DAUGHTERS... THIS WAS MY POPPI'S BLESSING AND HIS CURSE. I WAS THE YOUNGEST. HE TREATED ME LIKE THE BOY THAT HE WISHED I WAS.

ALL THESE YEARS, AND HE DOESN'T CHANGE THE LOCK!

MAYBE HE'S WAITING FOR YOU TO COME BACK?

MAYBE, MINK ...I DON'T THINK SO.

HE TAUGHT ME HOW TO FIX CARS. HE SHOWED ME THE BUSINESS. HE WAS A GOOD FATHER.

BUT A GIRL NEEDS A MOTHER TO SHOW HER WHAT'S WHAT, AND MY MOTHER... SHE DIED WHEN I WAS BORN. I WOULDN'T HAVE KNOWN NOTHING, IF NOT FOR MAGDALENA.

THIS WAY. IT ISN'T FAR.

SHE TOOK ME TO HER HEART, LIKE I WAS HER OWN FLESH, AND SHE KNEW WHAT WAS WHAT.

DON'T GO, SARITA! THIS DAVE IS NO GOOD. THE SMELL OF EVIL IS AROUND HIM.

MAGDALENA KNEW... A BAD MAN IN A QUIANA SHIRT COULD HAPPEN.

DON'T YOU EVER THINK OF LEAVING HOME? I COULD TAKE YOU PLACES... SHOW YOU THINGS... THINGS YOU'VE NEVER DREAMT OF.

THAT HOMBRE PROMISED ME THE MOON. HE GAVE ME THE NIGHT...

LOOK AT ME. I WANT TO SEE MY-SELF IN YOUR EYES!

THAT'S THE SMELL OF MOTOR OIL, MOMMI. I CAN NEVER GET IT OUT FROM MY NAILS. AND ANYWAYS, WE'RE JUST GOING TO THE DANCE-O-RAMA. ACROSS THE STREET! WHAT COULD HAPPEN SO CLOSE?

YES. I WOULD LIKE THIS VERY MUCH.

...THE NIGHT, THE HUNGER, AND THE GRAVE.

MY DAUGHTER! MY BABY GIRL!

I'M SORRY...SO, SO SORRY...

IT IS A STRANGE THING, SENSING THOSE YOU LOVE, AS THEY BEND TO DROP HOT TEARS ON YOUR CORPSE. AND YOU...TRAPPED, AWAKE AND UNDEAD, IN THE PRISON OF ICY FLESH... UNABLE TO CALL OR TO COMFORT THEM.

THEY BURN, THOSE TEARS. THE RIVERS IN HELL ARE MADE OF THEM.

HERE...GO IN HERE...UP THE STAIRS.

COULD I RETURN FROM HELL? COULD I FIND COMFORT IN A MOTHER'S ARMS?

MAYBE HOWLER WAS RIGHT. WE SHOULD...

QUIEN ES? SARITA ESTA MUERTA...

MAGDALENA! ABRE LA PUERTA! SOY YO, SARITA! ABRE, POR FAVOR!

PUHM PUHM

MADRE DE DIOS!

I CAN SEE SHE'S GONNA BE A LOTTA HELP.

116

COP...

SKREEEEEEEEEE

...ANOTHER RUN-IN WITH THE LAW.

CAN I HELP YOU, OFFICER?

PUH-DUHM! PUH-DUHM!

...BUT NEW YORK STATE'S GOT A HELMET LAW.

PUH-DUHM! PUH-DUHM! PUH-D

WELL, OFFICER, I DON'T THINK MUCH A' YOUR STATE, AN' I THINK EVEN LESS A' HELMETS...

YOUNG LADY, I DON'T KNOW WHAT THINGS ARE LIKE IN TEXAS...

...BUT, YOU LOOK REAL SWEET!

PUH-DUHM! PUH-DUHM!

UGHN!

WHAMP

PUH-DUHM!

PUH-DUHM! PUH-DUHM

NEW YORK OR DOWN IN TEXAS, BABE... SWEET DEATH, IT TASTES THE SAME!

I AM BACK FROM THE DEAD, AND MY MOTHER...SHE EMBRACES ME. SHE WILL HELP ME...HELP US...IF NOT TO LIVE, THEN TO CONTINUE.

THAT'S IT... WRITE IT THREE TIMES...

...THEN GIVE IT TO THE NEXT, AND *SHE* WILL WRITE THE NAME THREE TIMES.

YOUR TURN, MINK.

I'M NOT DONE WITH MY TOENAILS, YET. ALMOST.

HERE, SCREECH. PASS IT TO ME.

MAGDALENA IS SANTERA. SHE DOES WORKINGS. CONJURES.

NOW, PUT THE NAIL CLIPPINGS IN THE JAR...THAS RIGHT...PUT THEM IN AND THINK OF YOUR FEET WALKING FAR AWAY.

THIS WORKING, I GET FROM MY HAITIAN FRIEND, MONIQUE. SHE IS VOODOO-TRAINED...

...BUT WE ARE MUCH THE SAME. SO, I FILL THIS JAR WITH THE MAGNETIC SAND. THE SAND WILL CALL TO THIS DAVE... REACH INTO HIS GUT, TO PULL AT HIM.

MAGNETIC SAND

THIS JAR WILL DRAW THE EVIL ONE AWAY FROM YOU.

NOW...YOU MUST WRITE THE THING THAT YOU WANT, MY DAUGHTER.

THE THING THAT I *WANT.* WHAT IS THIS THING? TO *LIVE*...TO SEE THE *DAY*... TO WAKE ONCE *MORE,* IN MY *OWN* BED, AND IN MY *FATHER'S* HOME?

I WRITE, INSTEAD, THE THING I *NEED.*

HERE, MOMMI.

NOW...I MUST *BATHE* THE EGG IN THE *COMPELLING* OIL...

...AND *PLACE* IT INTO THE *JAR...*

...AND *SEAL* IT.

YOU MUST TAKE THE JAR, AND THROW IT INTO THE *WATER,* SO THAT IT IS CARRIED FAR AWAY FROM YOU. THE MAN WILL FOLLOW THE JAR, AND BE THINKING THAT HE FOLLOWS *YOU.*

PUH-DUHM! PUH-DUHM!

LESS THAN ONE HOUR BEFORE THE DAWN, BUT THE MORNING WILL *NOT* FIND ME IN MY FATHER'S HOUSE. THE HUNGER RISES IN ME...

...TURNED TO *ANIMAL* NEED, BY THE MUSIC OF THIS GOOD WOMAN'S HEART.

GOOD-BYE, MY DAUGHTER... GO WITH GOD!

NO, MOMMI, NEVER WITH *HIM...*

PUH-DUHM! PUH-DUHM!

119

DAMN! SKY'S LIGHTER. I CAN ALMOST *TASTE* THOSE BITCHES...DAMN CLOSE, NOW...

WELL, WELL, WELL... ASK AND YE SHALL RECEIVE, AND *RIGHT OFF THE HIGHWAY!*

BUT I BETTER TAKE THIS EXIT...LOOK FOR A PLACE TO SLEEP...

SAINT FRANCIS MEMORIAL GARDENS

MOTEL-8'S GOT NOTHIN' ON ME!

heh heh heh!

IT'S GOT NO CABLE, BUT WHAT THE HECK!

LADY WAGTAIL SWEET COMPANION BEST FRIEND

DAMN! I JUST CAN'T ESCAPE THE BITCHES! WELL, LASSIE...

...ROLL OVER!

IN THE HEIGHTS, THE MUCHACHOS, THEY RIDE ALL NIGHT. AROUND THE SAME EIGHT BLOCKS, THEY GO IN THEIR SOUPED-UP CARS... MERENGUE, AS LOUD AS THE END OF THE WORLD, BEATING THE BRAINS FROM THEIR HEADS.

JUST A LITTLE HIGHER, SUGAR.

C'MON, HURRY, POPPI! YOU'LL MISS THE PARTY!

ONE MINUTE, ONE MINUTE! I GOTTA LOCK MY CAR!

EARLIER, THESE NIÑOS, THEY WANTED TO GO OUT WITH US. NOW, THEY GO OUT FOR GOOD.

YOU NEVER HEARD OF CINDERELLA? YOU WAIT TOO LONG, YOU MISS THE BALL!

I POUR THE CANDY WORDS DOWN ON THIS BOY, COAXING THE PRINCE FROM HIS PUMPKIN...

...FOR THE SUN, HE POKES HIS HEAD OUT FROM THE BLANKET OF NIGHT. HIS RED HAIR STREAMS ACROSS THE PILLOW. WHEN HE WAKES, WE MUST BE SLEEPING.

I'M COMING, I'M COMING!

BUT FIRST, THERE IS THE HUNGER.

WHY DON'T YOU WAIT FOR ME, MOMMI? I THINK YOU DON'T--

HELP...HELP ME...

I AM SORRY, MI HERMANO. MAKE YOUR PRAYERS TO MARIA, IN HEAVEN...

...AND COME TO HELL WITH ME.

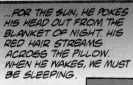

NEAR SUNRISE, UPSTATE NEW YORK:

JENN...CAN YOU *HEAR* ME, NOW? WE'RE CLOSE, SO CLOSE...

...YOU GOTTA *MAKE* IT...GOTTA *COME* TO ME!

'CAUSE YOU KNOW I CAN'T TAKE HIM, AND YOU HAVE TO DO IT FOR ME.

SLEEPY... CAN'T FADE... YOU HEAR ME, JENN?

GIRL, YOU'VE *GOTTA* HEAR.

A MONSTER CAN'T MOTHER A *CHILD.*

YES... YES, I HEAR.

WHAT'D YOU SAY, HON?

LOOKS LIKE WE'RE PRETTY NEAR...NEAR THE TOWN THAT POOR WOMAN TOLD US ABOUT. TAKE THAT RIGHT, UP AHEAD.

JENN, THIS DOESN'T LOOK LIKE THERE'S A TOWN ANYWHERE CLOSE, AN' I HAFTA ANSWER NATURE'S CALL...

...SO I'M JUST GON' PULL THE CAR OVER FOR A MINUTE.

YOU LOOK BEAT, HANK. HOW ABOUT I DRIVE FOR A WHILE?

SURE...SURE THING. I WANNA SEE THAT MAP, ANYWAY. FEELS LIKE WE MIGHTA MISSED A TURN BACK THERE.

I'M COMING, JEZZ...

VRRRUUUMMMMMMMM

...I'M COMING!

SO THE VAMPIRE'S *SISTER* DROVE OFF WITH YOUR WALLET? AND LEFT YOU IN THE MIDDLE OF NOWHERE? *MAN*, I HEARD OF GUYS HAVIN' *WOMEN* TROUBLE... BUT, WOMEN *VAMPIRES?!* THAT'S SOME STORY, PAL!

YEAH, I KNOW... PURTY UNBELIEVABLE.

GUESS I JUST WANTED SOMEBODY T'KNOW ABOUT IT, 'CASE I COME ACROSS 'EM IN A MEAN MOOD.

IF I HEAR OF ANY DEHYDRATED *PI*s FOUND IN A *DITCH* ON THE SIDE OF THE ROAD, I'LL ALERT THE AUTHORITIES. GOOD LUCK, HANK.

THANKS. AN' THANKS FOR THE RIDE.

HA HA HEE HEE HEE

WHAT A *WHACKO!*

...*VAMPIRES!*

WHAT KINDA TIME WE LOOKING AT?

WHIPSNAKE SAYS IT'S A BROKEN FUEL LINE... 'BOUT TWENTY MINUTES BROKEN.

HEY, SKEETER! WHY THE HELL D'JOO CHOOSE A SCOOT WITH A BUTTON IGNITION?

IT'S *HARD* TO KICK-START THE THING WHEN YOU'RE WEARIN' HIGH-*HEELS*...

...AN' I *LIKE* HIGH HEELS. THEY GIVE A PLEASIN' SHAPE TO THE LEG.

BEEP

EXCUSE ME, LADIES...

...ANY OF YOU KNOW WHERE I'D FIND THE GUY WHO'S RUNNING THE PLACE?

HE WAS HERE A FEW MINUTES AGO.

I THINK I REMEMBER HIM GOIN' OUT FOR A *NIBBLE*...

...OR MAYBE HE JUST *WENT* OUT?

MAYBE WE CAN HELP YOU?

RUH-DUHM PUH-DUHM

HELP YOU INTO YOUR NEXT LIFE!

DON'T WORRY, SWEETIE...

...WE'LL BE RE-E-E-E-AL NICE.

WHAT? HEY...HEY... WHAT! NO...

AIIIEEEEEE

RUH-DUHM RUH-DUHM PUH-DUHM

UGH...UGH...UGH... UGHHHHHHHN!

RUH-DUHM RUH-DUHM

SO...FIGURE I FIND 'EM. WHAT THE HECK AM I GON' DO THEN? MAKE A GODDAM *CITIZEN'S ARREST?* "FREEZE, LADIES! YOU'RE WANTED FOR BABY-NAPPIN'; GRAVE-ROBBIN', AN' SUCKIN' BLOOD ACROSS STATE LINES!"

CAN IT EVEN *BE* GRAVE-ROBBIN' IF THE CORPSE ROBS ITS OWN DANG GRAVE?

AN' WHAT IF JENN FINDS 'EM FIRST? SHE KNOWS WHERE THEY ARE, OR SHE WOULDN'A TOOK OFF LIKE THAT.

WILL BEIN' A MONSTER'S KIN BE ENOUGH TO KEEP HER SAFE?

JENNY...*DAMN!*

ARE YOU SURE IT'S *ME* YOU LOVE? NOT MY *SISTER?*

NO...IT'S *YOU*...IT'S *YOU*, JENN ...YOU...

BUT, IS THAT THE TRUTH? AND IS THERE REALLY ANY *DIFFERENCE*...

IS JENN BECOMING A... BECOMING ONE A' *THEM?*

I DON'T KNOW WHAT'S HAPPENING. I CAN'T SLEEP AT NIGHT AND THEN, IN THE DAY, ALL I *DO* IS SLEEP. I KEEP SEEING THESE *VISIONS*, HANK. I KEEP SEEING WHAT *SHE'S* SEEING! I SEE HER *TAKE* THEM...HER *VICTIMS!* I *FEEL* IT, HANK! I GET...I... IT MAKES ME FEEL ... *DRUNK* AFTER.

NO...NO... *NOOOOOO!*

I GET HIRED TO FIND A TRUCKER'S KILLER, AN' WHAT DO I FIND? PSYCHICS AN' DEAD INDIANS AN' VAMPIRES AN' CHILD STEALERS AND GOD-KNOWS-WHAT-ALL! NO WONDER BEDGOOD FIRED ME...

128

YOU THINK YOU'RE IMMORTAL, BUT I'LL GIVE THE LIE TO THAT.

'CAUSE I FEEL YOU FEMALES...

...LIKE A HORNY DOG FEELS A BITCH IN HEAT!

AND, I WILL SNIFF YOU OUT AND HUNT YOU DOWN, 'CAUSE, BITCHES? YOU CAN'T HIDE FROM OLE DAVE!

NO MORE'N A HALF-CHEWED BONE CAN HIDE FROM THE DOG THAT BURIED IT! I TOOK YOU OUT OF THE EARTH, AND I CAN PUT YOU RIGHT BACK...

...HUH?

AGGGGHH!

BACKLASH

ELAINE LEE — WRITER
WILLIAM SIMPSON — ARTIST
STUART CHAIFETZ — COLORIST
CLEM ROBINS — LETTERER
JULIE ROTTENBERG — ASS'T EDITOR
STUART MOORE — EDITOR
VAMPS CREATED BY ELAINE LEE AND WILLIAM SIMPSON

HELL HATH NO FURY LIKE AN S.O.B.'S BEEN DRAWN, QUARTERED, AN' STAKED THROUGH THE HEART BY THE FIVE VAMPS HE "TURNED."

DAVE CATCHES UP TO ME, HE'LL SPIT ME ON A PHONE POLE AN' LEAVE MY SORRY ASS T'COOK IN THE MORNIN' SUN.

MY ONLY HOPE'S HE'LL GET THE OTHER FOUR FIRST... KILL 'EM REAL SLOW... GIMME TIME T'FIND MY BOY... AN' JENN TIME T'FIND ME.

JENN, YOU COMIN'? YOU HEAR ME NOW, GIRL? GET YOUR REAR IN GEAR, SIS, 'CAUSE I GOT A NEED FOR FAMILY ...IN FLESH AS WELL AS IN BLOOD!

ONE THING I KNOW, JENN...VAMPS DON'T MAKE GOOD MAMAS. IT'S DAMN HARD TO FIND TIME FOR GYMBOREE, BETWEEN THE NIGHTS OF KILLIN' AND THE DEATH-SLEEP IN THE GRAVE ALL DAY.

AN' BABIES, THEY WAKE WITH THE LIGHT!

30

I TAKE MY LIGHT BOTTLED...FLUORESCENT OR SOFT WHITE OR HALOGEN HEADS. THAT PORCH LIGHT AHEAD SAYS, "TAKE ME."

ROSE LANE... RIGHT ROAD... MUST BE THAT HOUSE.

DAMN!

THEY STEAL MY BABY AN' SEND HIM T' LIVE WITH TRAILER TRASH? WHATEVER THESE FOLKS PAID, I COULDA MATCHED IT!

SEEMS LIKE A NICE GUY, THOUGH...GOOD DAD. HOW MANY KIDS...?

WHO'S MY FAVORITE BABY? WHO IS IT? WHO IS IT?

HEE-HEE-HEE-HEE HEE!

IS IT ME, DADDY? IS IT ME?

IT'S ME! IT'S ME! IT'S ME!

ALL GIRLS...

MUST BE THE HOUSE ACROSS THE ROAD.

I IGNORE THE SMELL OF LIQUID LIFE...THE HUNGER GNAWING IN MY GUT. SO, LAUGH, SWEET BABIES. DEATH BRINGS NO TEARS TO THIS HOUSE.

NOT TONIGHT.

I TURN T'GO, AN' DEATH DOGS MY FOOT-STEPS...JUST AS SHE'S DONE SINCE TH' NIGHT DAVE TURNED ME.

I'LL HELP YOU, JEZZ. YOU'LL NEVER BE HURT AGAIN.

I KNOW DEATH'S A WOMAN, 'CAUSE SHE HATES TO BE CHEATED...

JENN!

BE COOL, JEZZ...

...YOU DON'T WANT TO *FRIGHTEN* THE CHILD.

IT'S *TRUE*, JEZZZZ THE VISIONS ...THE BOY... WHAT YOU'VE *BECOME*?

ALL TRUE. I NEED YOU TO ...TAKE HIM, JENN ...YOU'RE *FAMILY* ...HE'LL KNOW ME THROUGH YOU.

GO ON UP TO YOUR ROOM, TOMMY...

GET THAT, WILLYA!

R-RING

IS THERE A *T*? D-DI-DING! YES! THREE *T*S!

YOU WANNA SOLVE NOW, OR SPIN AGAIN?

I'LL SPIN. VRR-RP-RP C'MON C'MON C'MON...

WHATTA THEY *WANT*, GRACE?

THREE HUNDRED!... ...I'D LIKE TO BUY AN *O*, PLEASE?... GIVE US AN *O*, PLEASE... **DI-DING!** ...TWO *O*'S!

IT'S FOR YOU.

ALL RIGHT, ALL RIGHT...I'M COMING...

I'D LIKE TO SOLVE, PLEASE...

..."BLOOD IS THICKER THAN WATER"!... YOU GOT IT!

YES? WHO'S...

YOU HIT THE CHILD.

YOU WILL NEVER HIT A CHILD AGAIN.

MAN, I'M BEAT. CAIN'T BE MUCH FURTHER. FOLKS SCARED A' HITCHHIKER'S THESE DAYS.

CAIN'T BLAME 'EM. MUST LOOK LIKE HELL.

VVVVRRRR

WHAT'S THAT? SOMETHIN' COMIN'? DON'T SEE ANY--

RRRRROOOOMMM

YAGHH!

NO LIGHTS!

VVRROOOOOMMM

UGHN!

VVROOM!

SHIT.

VRRRRMMMMMMMMM

YOU OKAY, BUDDY? CRAZY GIRLS PASSED ME BACK DOWN THE ROAD THERE! NEED A LIFT?

YEAH...YEAH, THANKS.

...THEM. THAT WAS THEM!

JETTER OUT HERE, OFF THE ROAD...LESS NOISE...I GET A BETTER READING, BABY. OLE DAVE'S GOTCHA ON HIS RADAR SCREEN. SOON, BABY, SOON!

SHHMUPT

AGHHHK!

OH, MAN! OH, MAN! I AM SO SORRY! DAMN! I THOUGHT YOU WERE A DEER!

OH...THINK NOTHING OF IT, FRIEND. I SHOULD'VE BEEN WEARING REFLECTIVE CLOTHING.

THWOK!

DAMN CRAZY HUNTER. COULDA HURT SOMEBODY!

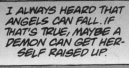

I ALWAYS HEARD THAT ANGELS CAN FALL. IF THAT'S TRUE, MAYBE A DEMON CAN GET HER- SELF RAISED UP.

MOMMY?

MAYBE, IF SHE BIRTHS AN ANGEL, HE COULD LIFT HER UP TO HEAVEN ON WINGS OF MORNING LIGHT.

THIS IS YOUR *REAL* MOMMY. SHE'S COME TO TAKE YOU TO A WONDERFUL PLACE.

A WONDER- FUL PLACE.

WHAT PLACE?

A PLACE WHERE LITTLE BOYS ARE NEVER, NEVER HURT...

NEVER HURT.

...A PLACE WHERE MOMMIES *PROTECT* THEIR CHILDREN, AND ALL THE DADDIES ARE KIND.

COULD WE TRY IT, ANGEL? COULD WE GIVE HEAVEN A TRY?

WE HAVE THREE NEW PUPPIES THERE AND A WHOLE POND FULL OF DUCKS. AUNT JEZZ AND I HAVE COME TO TAKE YOU THERE, SWEETHEART.

HELLO, TOMMY. I'M YOUR...AUNT JEZZ.

PUPPIES.

IF YOU'RE MY REAL MOMMY...

...IS THAT MY REAL *DADDY*?

GO ON, JENN ...TELL 'IM ABOUT HIS DADDY. THEN, TELL 'IM ALL ABOUT HIS *AUNT JEZZ.*

YOU KNOW IT. WON'T WORK, JENN. IT WAS WRONG A' THOSE MEN T'TAKE THE BOY, BUT TWO WRONGS DON'T MAKE A RIGHT. THESE PEOPLE...

THESE *PEOPLE* ARE LESS FIT TO BE PARENTS THAN *I* AM, BUDDY.

TAKE TOMMY UPSTAIRS AND PACK HIS THINGS.

THINGS.

MAYBE HEAVEN'S JUST A BIG RESTRICTED COUNTRY CLUB: NO LOW-RENT, CYCLE-RIDIN', UNWED, HOOKER VAMPIRES NEED APPLY.

WELL...IF THEY WON'T LET ME INTO HEAVEN...

AN' AS LONG AS WE'RE MOUTHIN' CLICHÉS, HOW 'BOUT "DEAD MEN TELL NO TALES"?

...I'LL HAVE TA TAKE 'EM WITH ME T'HELL.

WAIT! YOU DON'T HAVE TO KILL HANK.

YOU'D CHOOSE DUDLEY DORIGHT OVER YOUR OWN FLESH 'N BLOOD? THAT'S YOUR CROTCH TALKIN', JENN.

HE'S TOO RIGHTEOUS. HE'LL NEVER LEAVE US IN PEACE.

LOOK...TOMMY NEEDS YOU, SIS. BUT IF YOU'RE NOT UP TO IT...

I NEED TOMMY AS MUCH AS HE NEEDS ME.

I CAN'T HAVE ANY OF MY OWN, HANK. BUT...TO HAVE MY TWIN'S CHILD...GENETICALLY AND SPIRITUALLY, IT *WOULD* BE MINE! I ALREADY FEEL LIKE HE *IS* MINE...LIKE I GREW HIM INSIDE ME!

I LOVE YOU, JENNY. I THINK YOU KNOW THAT. AN' I KNOW YOU'RE BEIN' INFLUENCED...THAT YOU'RE NOT ...YOURSELF. BUT, *THIS?* THIS IS WRONG, JENN. AN' IF YOU SEARCH YOUR HEART, YOU'LL KNOW IT'S WRONG.

KILL HIM.

WELL, WELL, WELL...

A WOMAN AFTER MY *OWN HEART*... SUCH AS IT IS. I COULD ALMOST *FORGIVE* YOU FEMALES FOR CAUSIN' ME SO MUCH TROUBLE. OR...

...I COULD *SCREW* FORGIVENESS, AND KILL THE RUG RAT.

WHA...?

CATCH!

OH, THE ACHE! A TENDERNESS STRONGER THAN THE BLOOD LUST OR DEATH. MY BOY! MY LIVING HEART!

WHAT'RE YOU, HUMAN? MOTHER'S LITTLE HELPER?

SOME DEAD, HARD PART OF ME CRACKS...

SAY "GOOD NIGHT," MISTER MAN!

...AND, THROUGH THAT FISSURE IN MY MONSTER SOUL, SOMETHING NEARLY HUMAN BREAKS.

RUN, JENN!

JENN... I'LL COME AFTER YOU...

YOU WON'T FIND US.

HOW MANY TIMES DO I HAVE TO KILL YOU, YOU SHIT?!

KRASH

143

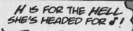

H IS FOR THE *HELL* SHE'S HEADED FOR ♪!

I TURNED YOU, BABE. I'M THE STRONGER. AS A PAL OF MINE USED TO SAY... "I'M THE *KING* AND YOU'RE *NOTHIN'*!"

NOW, IF THAT'S CLEAR TO YOU...

E IS FOR THE *ENTRAILS* SHE'LL BE *TRAILING*! ♪ R IS FOR THE *RUG RAT*...

...AND, MAKE NO MISTAKE ABOUT IT, RED, I'LL KILL HIM ONCE I'M DONE WITH YOU!

PUT THEM ALL *TOGETHER*, THEY SPELL *MOTHER*...! ♪

SSSHWWPT

AGHHK!

144

HOLY SHIT!

THUD!

DAVE, YOU DUMB CRACKER ...YOU NEVER COULD SING WORTH SHIT!

NOW THE POT IS CALLING THE SKILLET BLACK.

HELP ME PULL HER OFF HIM.

ICK!

NOTHING'S HAPPENING.

MMMM... WAKE UP AN' SMELL THE BLOOD PUMPIN', BABY. YOURS SMELLS GOOD.

FUH DMM! FUH DMM!

SOON...

THE *NICE* COUPLE THAT LIVES HERE WILL UNTIE YOU IN A COUPLA DAYS, HANK. YOU WON'T STARVE BEFORE THEN.

I LEFT 'EM ALIVE AS A FAVOR TO YOU...

...FOR SAVIN' MY BOY AN' ALL. SAME REASON I LET YOU LIVE.

MUCH OBLIGED.

OBLIGED.

JUST OUT OF CURIOSITY, WHATCHA GON' DO WITH YER BOYFRIEND?

LET'S JUST SAY WE CAN'T GET THE BASTARD OFF OUR *BACKS*, AN' LET IT GO AT THAT.

BACKS.

HE'S IN YOUR *BACKPACK'S*? YOU GON' DROP HIM OFF THE SIDE A' THE ROAD, THEN, PUT A FEW MILES BETWEEN THE PIECES THIS TIME? WHAT ABOUT *AFTER* THAT...YOU PLANNIN' TO MEET YOUR SISTER SOMEWHERE? HER AND THE BOY?

LISTEN. YOU GO AFTER JENN AN' MY BOY,..YOU EVEN *TRY* T'FIND 'EM...AN' I'LL HUNT YOU DOWN AND KILL YOU IN THE MEANEST WAY I CAN.

THEN, I'LL COME BACK HERE AN' KILL THESE SONS-A-BITCHES AN' TAKE MY BOY BACK, AGAIN.

I WOULDN'T HURT YOUR SISTER. I JUST WANNA KNOW SHE'S OKAY... THAT YOU HAVEN'T DONE NOTHIN' *PERMANENT* TO HER.

NO, JENN'S FREE OF ME, NOW, LIKE I'M FREE OF JEZZ ...OF JEZZ AND HER PAST AND HER ENEMIES AND HER KIN. SO, DON'T GO HUNTIN' ME AT MY SISTER'S DOOR.

C'MON, SUGAR' ENGINE'S RUNNIN'!

YOU SURE YOU DON'T WANNA UNTIE ME? I'LL BE REAL GOOD ...I SWEAR...

DON'T PRESS YOUR LUCK, BABY.

146

YOU *KNOW* I'LL HAVE TO COME LOOKIN' FOR YA!?

I'LL HAVE TO *FIND* YOU!

YOU DON'T *WANNA* FIND US, SUGAR!

BUT IF YOU *DO*...

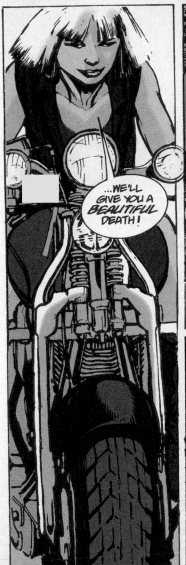

...WE'LL GIVE YOU A *BEAUTIFUL* DEATH!

HOW DO THE OTHERS STAND IT? THIS LONELINESS, THIS STANDING OUTSIDE OF LIFE? IT'S WORSE FOR THEM, THAN FOR ME.

THE CHILD OF MY HUMAN FLESH AND JENNY, MY TWIN...WHO SHARES MY VERY GENES. WHILE THEY LIVE, PART OF ME LIVES.

148

149

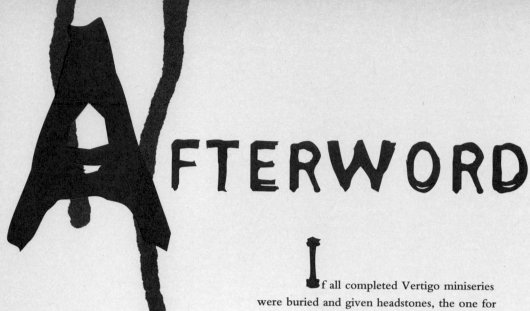

AFTERWORD

If all completed Vertigo miniseries were buried and given headstones, the one for Vamps would read: VAMPS, 1994-1994, "They Loved It. They Hated It. They Bought It."

Yes, they bought it. So, now I've been asked to write my own afterword to the collected VAMPS, when I haven't really had time to be sure what I think about it. One thing I do know... those who bought it and read it know *exactly* how they feel about it. And, I know how they feel, because they *let* me know. They wrote to me, and they sent E-mail, and they told other people who then told me.

I'm not sure why the reaction was so extreme but, judging from the mail and the on-line response, this wasn't a series that folks felt so-so about. Some hated it but felt compelled to buy it. Some loved it but felt guilty about loving it, the letters reading as though the fans were confessing to having carnal knowledge of a family member. Some of the letters we've received from male readers questioned whether this story of feminine evil wasn't just a tad sexist (one called it an "adolescent anti-female wet dream"), and some said they might be insulted if they were women. At the same time, the letters we received from actual women were unanimously positive. They got off on the powerful female characters, evil or no. Many of the men did too, implying they would gladly die with smiles on their faces, given the chance to bed a Vamp. Then, there were those who read the same series as a radical feminist rant against men. All of these people read the same story. Could it be that there is something about the material that sets fire to the attitudes the readers bring to it?

By Elaine Lee

I'm reminded, in fact, of a cartoon that I found in a local college newspaper and pinned to my office wall. In this cartoon, three men stand in an art gallery, before a sculpture of a nude female torso. The first man is thinking, "Smut!" The second is thinking, "Art!" And, the third man is thinking, "An insult to headless quadriplegics!"

We'll admit to this much... VAMPS is violent. VAMPS is sexy. VAMPS is about five women, with supernatural powers, who feed on men to live. It is, after all, a vampire story. But, readers, who seem to have accepted the mix of violence and sex in the more traditional stories of male vampires, were very much bothered by it in the VAMPS series. Why is this? Through countless films and retellings, Dracula's female victims have writhed in filmy nighties on satin-draped beds, moaning, "Yes, Master! Take me, Master!", as the Count from Transylvania has his deadly way with them. And, though Ms. Rice's male vampires seem to prefer both the company and the blood of men, the scenes of their unholy communion are unmistakably sexual. Whether they feed upon the same sex or the opposite, male vampires are allowed their deadly hunger and are loved all the more for it. Female vampires must be punished. Even the wonderfully conscienceless Claudia is destroyed early on in the popular Vampire Chronicles, while male characters sin but are forgiven.

Is it simply that the Vamps are women? Or is it that they are women who get away with it? There have been, after all, many other female vampires. But, the Vamps aren't beheaded, staked, or burned within minutes of their first appearance, as are most of Dracula's victim-vampires. They aren't mindless graveyard wraiths. They aren't ultimately saved from themselves, either through the power of love or by the power of Almighty God. Instead, with a promise of easy sex, they lure young men out of bedrooms, bars, and vehicles and drain them of their blood, touch up their lipstick, and take off down the road. They feel no remorse. And they provoke the same reaction that Lorena and her knife, Louise and her revolver, and Glenn and her dead bunny, provoked before them. For men, they pose the question, "Do you really *know* that woman you've let get into that bed with you?" Some men can face that question. Others can't.

Bluntly stated, any vampire story is rape fantasy without guilt. The vampire takes what he wants and the victim has little to say about it. But, we're allowed to be excited by it because, hey... it's all fantasy. There's no such thing as a vampire, after all. Even if there were, could a dead guy get his equipment to work? Most vamp mythographers say, "no." But, don't kid yourselves, it's still rape fantasy... a heady mix of power and sex and death. And a story in which a female vampire feeds on male victims is reverse rape fantasy. The man has it done to him. Some men are revolted by that, some are turned on. "Just lay back and enjoy it, Sugar" purr the Vamps, for they are anything but politically correct.

So, you can all stop speculating on why I might have written VAMPS (Is she a radical lesbian with a feminist agenda? Is she a female Uncle Tom, with nothing but heteroS-E-X on the brain?), because I'm going to tell you. I wanted to do a modern vampire story, with characters who were like myself and like some of the crazy, wild women I've known. What if I became a vampire? Or Augusta? Or Cal?

The story begins where I began (in North Carolina) and ends up where I've ended up (in New York). Skeeter is my wild child self... the one that left a string of broken hearts and shattered psyches across several states, while still in her early twenties. She's the Southern Belle I used to be, was born in the year that I was born, and is the part of me that wishes I could still be twenty but "know what I know now." Mink is the would-be movie star, with the huge blonde ego. In my later twenties, I was an actress in daytime drama, and Mink gets her hair color and choice of professions from that part of me. Screech is the urban artist... the part of myself that let me be lured away from the soaps, into the exciting (and much less profitable) world of fringe comics. I made her Chinese as a tribute to my friend, Sharon, who nursed me through Vertigo's long approval process. Whipsnake is my old neighborhood in Washington Heights, the result of thirteen years of constant merengue music, pounding out of boom boxes and car speakers, to filter through my brain. Finally, Howler is my good-old-gal self, the part of me that finally left the city to spend my winters slogging through the mud and snow upstate. She had a beautiful boy child. So did I. The great thing about aging is that you have the opportunity to invent yourself again and again, and each of the Vamps contains a bit of me... the worst bits. They also contain pieces of all the women I've ever howled with.

Once upon a night, back in 1986, five hot women got dressed to the nines and went to a belly dancing club in Manhattan. I was one of them. The club catered to foreign diplomats from the U.N. and was very pricy, so we had a slice of pizza across the street before going in, and saved our money to buy champagne. We needn't have bothered. We were the only table of women in the club. Men began to send us bottles of champagne... Japanese men, German men, Russian men... their linen-covered tables dotting the floor of the club like tiny nations. And we watched the dancers and drank champagne, and were sent more champagne, which we also drank while watching more dancers. Then *we* danced and the men bought us more champagne. Then a hefty male belly dancer from Egypt, who had just bought us champagne (after Helen had goaded him into dancing for us), said something piggy about "women's place," and that made Calliope mad and she challenged the guy to arm wrestle. We cleared away the empty bottles, they faced off, and she beat him. In front of his friends. He was good-natured enough to forgive us and we were just drunk enough to give him our phone numbers. Then, after peeling several men off us, we piled into a cab with a Haitian driver, who cured Augusta's champagne stomach by sticking a broken twig behind her ear. He told us it was Voodoo. The next day Gamal the belly dancer called us.... all five of us. Some of us even remembered who he was.

Now, I could have told you about the night of upside-down Margaritas that put Susan in the hospital, or the time Augusta and I tried to skin a deer we'd found dead in the road, or about any one of a number of Halloweens, but I think you get the picture. All of my friends are Vamps. I wrote the book for them, and for all the women like them, and for all the men who love that kind of woman. That said, I'll mention some of them by name...

For Ruth, who once put a beer mug through the bar mirror in BJ's Saloon, because all the cute men she met turned out to be gay. She couldn't help it. She's an Aries.

For Augusta, who left a good job at a major fashion magazine to drive around North America in a van with Mary Thunder and sing at sweat lodge ceremonies.

For Ellen, who once left a party to run "buck naked" around the block, on a dare. (I was at the party and that's all that I'll admit to.)

For Jeanne, Isadora's torchbearer, who blindfolded her tour group and made them crawl through a labyrinth in Crete, there to wrestle with Minotaurs.

For Calliope, swordswoman and entrepreneur, who ran away from home at the age of fourteen and not only survived, but excelled.

For Karen, who slept with every male member of all three casts of *The Pirates of Penzance*. And my brother. And my sister. I think it's some kind of a record.

For Gabrielle, the gorgeous German runner, who spent her days writing her doctoral dissertation, and her nights dancing around pagan bonfires.

For Barbara, who asked me to photograph the birth of her son, and rewarded me by giving birth while the doctor was taking his coffee break.

And for the lady whose lace panties ended up in my mother's swimming pool filter. I'm not sure who you are, but I've narrowed it down to one of five.

Elaine Lee
Manhattan

ALSO AVAILABLE FROM TITAN

BLACK ORCHID
(W) Gaiman (A) McKean

THE BOOKS OF MAGIC
(W) Gaiman (A) various

THE BOOKS OF MAGIC: BINDINGS
(W) Rieber (A) Amaro/Gross

DEATH: THE HIGH COST OF LIVING
(W) Gaiman (A) Bachalo/Buckingham

ENIGMA
(W) Milligan (A) Fegredo

THE SANDMAN: PRELUDES & NOCTURNES
(W) Gaiman (A) Kieth/Dringenberg/M. Jones, III

THE SANDMAN: THE DOLL'S HOUSE
(W) Gaiman (A) Dringenberg/various

THE SANDMAN: DREAM COUNTRY
(W) Gaiman (A) various

THE SANDMAN: SEASON OF MISTS
(W) Gaiman (A) K. Jones/various

THE SANDMAN: A GAME OF YOU
(W) Gaiman (A) McManus/various

THE SANDMAN: BRIEF LIVES
(W) Gaiman (A) Thompson/Locke

THE SANDMAN: FABLES AND REFLECTIONS
(W) Gaiman (A) various

THE SANDMAN: WORLDS' END
(W) Gaiman (A) various

V FOR VENDETTA
(W) A. Moore (A) Lloyd

COMING SOON

THE SANDMAN: THE KINDLY ONES